Sweet
Sabotage

K.D. McCrite

Annie's®
AnniesFiction.com

Books in the Chocolate Shoppe Mysteries series

Library of Congress-in-Publication Data
Sweet Sabotage / by K.D. McCrite
p. cm.
I. Title
                    2017944658

AnniesFiction.com
(800) 282-6643
Chocolate Shoppe Mysteries™
Series Creator: Shari Lohner
Series Editors: Janice Tate, Ken Tate
Cover Illustrator: Bonnie Leick

10 11 12 13 14 | Printed in South Korea | 9 8 7 6 5 4 3 2

Bertie Harper hung up the telephone behind the counter and stood frozen, fingers still resting on the handset, gaze fixed on the wall.

Jillian Green turned from making fresh coffee. Her heart pounded as she watched color drain from her grandmother's face. The pallor and frozen expression were unlike Bertie's usual energetic, healthy appearance.

"Bertie, what's wrong? Are you all right?"

When the woman remained silent, eyes glazed, Jillian's mind squirmed with unwanted notions. Had something happened to her great-aunt Cornelia, Bertie's twin sister? Was something wrong at Belle Haven, the huge antebellum mansion the three of them called home? Maybe one of their many friends was sick, or injured, or worse. Jillian touched her grandmother's arm and got no reaction.

"Bertie? Who was that on the phone? What's happened?"

Lenora Ryan, Bertie's indispensable right hand at The Chocolate Shoppe, emerged from the kitchen, her dark face becoming a mask of concern when she saw Bertie's expression. She wiped her hands on a towel.

"What's going on?" she said.

"I don't know," Jillian said. "She hasn't moved since the phone call."

Lenora's forehead creased. She snapped her fingers two inches in front of Bertie's face. The woman started and blinked.

"What's the matter with you, snapping your fingers at me like a mud turtle?" Anytime Bertie became irritable with anyone other than her sister, worry was the foundation.

"I never knew a mud turtle had fingers," Lenora growled back, "but I reckon if that's what you want to think, go ahead. What's wrong with you anyhow, standing there gawking into space like that and scaring Jillian and me? If you're fixin' to have a spell, I'll call for an ambulance right now."

"Oh, for pity's sake, I'm not having a spell, and you know it." Bertie flapped both hands, shooing the two women back. "I've never had a spell in my life."

"What's wrong?" Jillian asked. "Who was on the phone?"

Bertie shot a gaze around the bakery. "Where is everyone? Every blessed table is empty, and we haven't had but a handful of customers since the morning rush."

Jillian glanced at the clock. "We hardly ever have more than a handful of customers at two in the afternoon, especially on a Monday. And with the whole country on a health kick, not many people eat doughnuts and cream-filled Long Johns for lunch. We'll get the after-school crowd in about an hour as usual." She tried to peer into her grandmother's bright-blue eyes, but Bertie scowled at her and turned away.

"You've never worried about light traffic at this time of day," Lenora said.

"We've never had serious competition before."

Lenora and Jillian exchanged glances. "Competition?" they chorused.

Bertie nodded and made her way to the nearest table where she sank heavily into one of the chairs. "That was Wanda Jean Maplewood on the phone."

The tight band inside Jillian relaxed a bit. She prepared to hear a crazy rumor and a bit of highly exaggerated gossip. "I wouldn't take anything Wanda Jean might have to say too seriously."

Bertie didn't even look at her. "You know the new construction going up over there near the high school?"

Of course they knew about it. Moss Hollow had been astounded, alarmed, and abuzz ever since learning that Guy & Ginger's had been bought out a few weeks ago and was scheduled for demolition. Guy & Ginger's had been on the corner lot of Catalpa and Maple long before Jillian was born. Kitty-corner from the high school, the compact, square little neighborhood market used to sell everything from rice to live bait to paperback romance novels to screwdrivers. Two huge oak trees with gray-green Spanish moss dripping from their massive branches had shaded the store for longer than anyone could remember.

Guy and Ginger Halstead had tended the store, along with their son, Junior, until they were in their nineties. Junior's three kids moved away as soon as they were grown, and with no interest in Moss Hollow or the store, they rarely returned. After he passed away, the building sat unused, fading, like an impoverished and aging Southern belle.

"Guess what it's going to be?" Bertie asked.

"If Wanda Jean Maplewood told you about it, then it'll probably be a brand-new international airport," Lenora said. "Or a diamond mine."

Jillian snorted.

Bertie rolled her eyes. "She swears up, down, and sideways her news is true."

"So what did she say was coming? A casino?" Jillian asked. She couldn't imagine anything that might get under her grandmother's skin more than a place where people lost their hard-earned money on foolishness.

"Another convenience store?" Lenora asked. "Seems like we got more convenience stores than we can use in this town. Why would we need another?"

Bertie huffed. "You two beat all. No casino, thank heaven, and not another convenience store, though either one would be preferable to what's coming."

"Will you stop dillydallying and tell us what it is?" Lenora demanded.

"It's going to be Moss Hollow's own Confections & Donuts."

"*What?*"

Confections & Donuts, the popular national chain of bakeries, was scattered across the country and sold every kind of sweets from pastries to divinity. Moss Hollow was known for small, family-owned businesses, and everyone wanted to keep it that way. Or so Jillian thought.

If Wanda Jean's news is true, apparently not everyone wants to stay small and cozy.

"You know what that means, don't you?" Bertie said. "They'll wipe The Chocolate Shoppe Bakery right off the face of the map. We'll lose everything."

"Wait a minute," Jillian said. "Think about where you got your information."

"Wanda Jean said Maudie told her."

Jillian let out a long breath as her middle relaxed even more. "Okay, Bertie, let's not get upset just yet. You know as well as I do that those two women are the biggest gossips in Moss Hollow, if not all of Nathan County."

"That's right," Lenora said, nodding vigorously. "If they can't find anything to gossip about, they'll make it up."

"But she said Maudie got word from a reliable source."

"I'll bet." Lenora took a clean cloth and began polishing the glass on the display case.

Jillian grabbed one of Bertie's hands. It trembled in her grasp. The Chocolate Shoppe had been a Moss Hollow institution for nearly as long as Jillian could remember. It was Bertie's lifeblood.

"Listen to me. Nothing is going to happen to the bakery. Let me ask around before you borrow trouble. Okay? I'll go right now."

"You might as well," Bertie said, running a gaze across her empty bakery. "There's nothing to keep you here."

Jillian knew no amount of consolation would stop this dear woman from worrying. The sooner Jillian could learn the facts and put Bertie's mind at rest, the better. She prayed this news was nothing but unfounded rumor.

"Listen to your girl," Lenora told Bertie. "She's got plenty of sense. Most of the time." She winked at Jillian.

"She gets that from me," Bertie sighed. She squeezed Jillian's hand then let go.

Jillian drove straight to the chamber of commerce office, which was housed in what could only be described as a shrunken replica of Scarlet O'Hara's beloved Tara. Square, white, with pillars on the front porch, the building was about the size of the average fast-food place. She opened the tall, white door and walked into an airy, high-ceilinged room decorated with a mixture of antique furniture and contemporary glass-topped tables.

Leslie Phipps, who frequently showed up at various agencies in town as an overeager volunteer, sat behind the reception desk. She looked up.

"Hi, Jillian!" Plump and cheerful, Leslie also possessed the annoying trait of talking in a stream of mindless chatter, flowing from subject to subject without logic or restraint. "I've been going over the new brochures that just arrived, but honestly, I don't see much difference between them and the ones we discontinued." She swept one hand back and forth. "Seems like a waste money. But then, I don't run the chamber, I just answer the phone and greet folks when they come in. We still use this old-style desk phone, cord and all." She patted it fondly. "Which I guess I should be grateful for, because otherwise it would be smartphones here at work just like everywhere else, which gets under my skin when I'm talking to someone and they start looking at their phone instead of paying attention to me. Does that bother you? Would you like some coffee? Or bottled water? We don't have sweet tea—would you believe it? Of course, there's the soda machine outside, which charges far too much. Do you remember when we were kids, you could buy a can of pop for what, forty or fifty cents?"

"I don't need anything to drink, Leslie. Thank you. I'd like to talk to Megan Farley."

"You would? What about?" One thing about Leslie, she never let common courtesy stand in her way. Her eyes sparkled with curiosity.

"Just something on behalf of my grandmother."

"Bertie Harper!" Leslie clasped her hands together as if thrilled. "I haven't seen her in a coon's age. I keep meaning to get over to The Chocolate Shoppe, but I went on this grapefruit diet. You eat nothing but grapefruit for six days. I've lost five pounds since Saturday. Before that I was on the cabbage soup diet, where you can have nothing but cabbage soup for a month, even breakfast. It was all right for a day or two, but I really couldn't see any significant weight loss by the third day. I loved the banana diet, where you eat nothing but bananas and fresh pineapple, but I gained twelve pounds before I found out it was a hoax. There are so many scams and hoaxes, you really have to be careful, don't you?" She ran a quick glance over Jillian. "You are so lucky you don't have to diet, Jillian. I don't understand why you aren't a regular li'l butterball, having all those lovely bakery treats to tempt you every day. How is your granny, anyway?"

"She's upset. That's why I need to talk with Megan." Jillian hoped the urgency in her voice would derail Leslie's prattle. Her ears were nearly ringing as it was.

"Megan upset Bertie? How?"

"Megan didn't upset Bertie, but I'm hoping she can give me a bit of information that will help to calm Bertie."

"Why? What's going on? You know you can tell me anything, because I have my finger right smack on the pulse of this town. That's one of the benefits of being here at the chamber. And I don't tell secrets. If someone says, 'Don't you breathe a word of this!' you can bet your boots I won't say a thing."

Fortunately for Jillian, Megan stepped out of her office. Tall and elegant in a tailored aubergine suit, her sandy-brown hair in a smooth upsweep, the woman looked as if she belonged in a corner suite on Wall Street rather than working as the executive director of the chamber of commerce in Moss Hollow, Georgia.

"I thought I heard a familiar voice, Jillian. How are you?" She crossed the room, right hand extended, her high heels clicking on the polished marble floor. As they shook hands, Jillian wondered why her voice was familiar to Megan when the two of them hardly knew each other.

"Good afternoon, Megan. I'm doing fine, but I wondered if I could bend your ear for a few minutes?"

"Certainly. Come into my office."

"Shall I bring y'all some coffee?" Leslie jumped up, as eager as a puppy. "I can make it fresh."

Megan raised one brow at Jillian.

"No thank you," Jillian said, keeping her voice polite even though she'd already told Leslie this.

"No coffee, Leslie. Jillian, this way." She led the way into the small, immaculate office and closed the door. "I'm so sorry you got cornered by Leslie. I do my best to run interference before she drives away visitors, but I'm not always successful. I'd dismiss her, but how can you fire a volunteer?" She indicated a plush white armchair. "Have a seat."

"She has good intentions," Jillian said. "She wants so much to be liked that she comes off too strong."

Megan settled behind her desk. "Do you know her well?"

"She was a couple of years behind me in school. She ran for various class and student body offices and joined every club she could, but she got on everyone's nerves. She tried too hard, bless her heart."

"Yes. Bless her heart." Megan's smile seemed forced. "Let's forget about Leslie, and you tell me what's on your mind."

"Guy & Ginger's."

Megan's smile slipped away completely. "That situation has stirred up quite a bit of controversy in town, hasn't it? The building is an eyesore, but the location is a prime piece of real estate. It was time for Guy & Ginger's to go."

Jillian tried not to let the words irritate her. "I know you've lived in Moss Hollow for a fairly short time, so you don't understand the attachment folks have to that place."

Megan waved one elegant hand. "Oh, please. I know all I need to know of the story, from the time it was built nearly a hundred years ago until now, and how people liked to congregate on that big porch and visit, and how they even did so for a while after Junior died. I can't tell you how many times I've heard about the four rocking chairs that were put in place on that porch the day the store opened and were never removed, not even after it went out of business. So what? Old buildings are torn down all the time in Atlanta."

Jillian curled her hands in her lap and leaned forward. "But this is not Atlanta. This is Moss Hollow, and losing Guy & Ginger's is like losing an old friend."

Megan gave her a chilly smirk. "In that case, the family and friends should have taken better care of the place while it was here. If one of the Moss Hollow citizens had bought and restored it, maybe we could do something about it."

Jillian's nails bit deeply into her palms. "Given the opportunity, that's likely what would have happened, but the first anyone knew the family no longer owned the store was when two huge *No Trespassing* signs went up a couple of weeks ago. The next thing we knew, a truck deposited an enormous Dumpster in front of the building and a crew filled it with everything left in the building. When folks showed up trying to find out what was going on, they were met by the construction foreman and told to leave."

"And your point is?"

Jillian sat back, staring at Megan's inexpressive face. Could the woman truly be as clueless and heartless as she seemed? If she was this indifferent about Moss Hollow, why was she the head of the chamber of commerce? What good could she possibly be to a town whose history and memories were precious to its citizens?

Jillian cleared her throat and forced herself to relax. "Actually, the reason I'm here is to help ease my grandmother's mind. She heard this morning that Confections & Donuts will be putting up one of their bakeries on the site. Is that true?"

Megan seemed frozen in place. Then she blinked. "Where did your grandmother hear that?"

"From a friend."

Megan gazed at her for several seconds, then turned to stare out the window next to her desk. "One can't help but wonder about small towns and the minds of those who inhabit them." She faced Jillian. "Who else knows?"

"So it *is* true."

Megan shifted in her chair and dropped her gaze. "I'm not saying that."

Jillian got to her feet. "You don't have to say it. Your face and body language speak for you."

Megan stood. She rested both hands on her desktop and leaned forward, meeting Jillian's eyes straight on.

"When I was hired, I was asked to help Moss Hollow thrive. Within the first day I saw how much this town needs to step out of the past and into the twenty-first century. Just like sitting on the front porch, visiting with neighbors and sipping sweet tea, the mom-and-pop stores have had their day. These businesses are unable to support themselves, let alone the families who own them. The buildings become run down and destroy the commercial value of the area in which they are located. They are a detriment to any town that tries to keep them. Like it or not, the world has turned corporate, Jillian. In order to flourish, Moss Hollow must follow."

Jillian's temperament was usually warm and understanding. She was rarely given to moments of unbridled anger, but right then she could hardly hear above the ringing in her ears. She wanted to throw something at the arrogant woman standing across the desk from her. She wanted to pitch a hissy fit, to shout, to break something. But her rearing had taught her that screaming at someone was both foolish and futile.

"I guess there's nothing left to say then." She stood to leave. At the door, she looked at Megan over her shoulder. "By the way, people in Moss Hollow still sit on the front porch with neighbors and sip sweet tea. Thank you for your time." She walked out of the office, shutting the door quietly behind her instead of slamming it hard enough to break the frame.

"Did you have a good visit?" Leslie said. "Megan isn't much for casual chatting, is she? But she certainly works hard. Why, she's on that computer or her phone all day, or checking out things in town. Sometimes, I walk past here at night, and the light is on in her office. She shouldn't work such long hours. It's hard on the heart, you know. I read an article the other day that more and more women are—"

Jillian held up one hand and smiled. "I'm sorry I can't stay, Leslie. But I will let you in on something that Megan may not want me to share." She leaned forward and whispered, "I think you should try to volunteer here more often than you do. I have a feeling she really, *really* gets something out of her chats with you."

Leslie's mouth and eyes rounded, then she grinned. "I bet that's why she gets that look on her face when we talk."

"No doubt."

"There is no one who knows more about Moss Hollow than me. I'll be sure to keep her informed."

"If I were you, I'd make sure she doesn't miss *any* of the news."

"I'll be sure to tell her. I absolutely will."

If guilt poked at her as she walked to her car, Jillian failed to feel it. But once her momentary surge of triumph subsided, worry over Bertie returned. Could The Chocolate Shoppe Bakery survive a big franchise like Confections & Donuts?

Not if Megan Farley is any indication, she thought. *How many more like her live in Moss Hollow?*

Jillian wanted to prepare herself for giving Bertie the bad news, so she put off going back to the bakery for a little while. She drove to the corner of Maple Street and Catalpa, to the empty lot where Guy & Ginger's stood awaiting its final destiny.

She parked and sat in the car, eyeing the place. Heavy equipment was parked to one side, ready for use. Her heart broke when she saw the uprooted oak trees. The buzz of several chain saws ripped the air, flinging debris from the downed trees as the teeth of the chains tore into what had been healthy, leafy, living branches an hour or two ago. Those trees were more than a century old and had shaded generations of Moss Hollow folks. Jillian wanted to weep as she gazed at the carnage.

How could this beloved little spot on the landscape change so dramatically in just one week?

No one in town had known that the family had put the place up for sale. Until Maudie had done some digging, no one knew who had bought it and for what purpose. Why all the secrecy surrounding this enterprise? Why had Megan Farley been so aggravated that the new business wasn't a secret? Could it be that she—

Someone rapped on the window next to her, and Jillian nearly jumped out of her skin.

A beefy man in a dark-blue security guard uniform stood next to the driver's door, scowling at her.

"What's your business?" he growled.

She blinked. "My business?"

"Why are you here?"

She pointed at the demolition going on. "I'm watching that."

He ran his gaze along her Prius, leaned forward to look around at the car's interior. He straightened but kept his eyes on her.

"You can't be here."

"What do you mean I can't be here?"

"I mean we don't want no troublemakers."

Jillian's mood had already been soured by Megan Farley. This man's attitude sent her closer to the edge. "This is a city street, a public place designated for parking, paid for with tax dollars. Of course I can be here."

A patrol car pulled up behind her and sat idling for a moment, then a deputy in sunglasses climbed out and strolled toward them. She recognized the tall form and swaggering walk, and groaned inwardly. *Gooder Jones.*

"What's the problem, Barry?" he asked.

The guard dipped his head toward Jillian. "She's trying to make trouble."

"I mostly certainly am not. Gooder, I am sitting here minding my own business and looking at Guy & Ginger's. Or what used to be Guy and Ginger's."

"When people play the 'I'm a taxpayer' card," the guard growled, "I know they're fixin' to start trouble."

"I did not play a card. I merely stated this is a public place, paid for by taxes. I wanted to look at this corner again before that awful new business goes up."

Gooder Jones pulled off his sunglasses, revealing green eyes that rarely softened. "What awful new business?"

"Confections & Donuts."

Both his eyebrows went up, as did the corners of his mouth. "No kidding? That's what they're putting here? I'd heard it was gonna be a radiator shop."

"Hey." The guard glowered, as if he'd drag both of them off the city street and into an alley. Antagonizing a deputy sheriff might not be the wisest move the man could make, seeing as Gooder had two inches and several pounds on him, not to mention a firearm strapped to his hip.

Gooder ignored him. "Guess Bertie's none too happy, huh?"

"She won't be when I give her the news."

The deputy focused his gaze on the workers. "Why are you looking at that mess, Jillian? Something in there you wanted?"

"No. I was just thinking of how it used to be when we were kids. Ice cream sandwiches, bubble gum, soda pop."

His face relaxed a little, and he nodded. "Peanuts and a bottle of Coke."

She grinned. "Remember the year everyone was wearing those denim jackets with the three pockets and the label on the sleeve, and this was the only place that sold them? Junior couldn't keep them in stock that year."

"Old MacDonald's, we called those jackets. I still have mine, somewhere."

Jillian raised an eyebrow at him. "Can you still fit into it?"

"Are you kidding?"

They laughed and the guard shifted impatiently.

"So, are you fixin' to cause trouble, Jillian?" Gooder asked.

"*No.*" She glared at the guard. "I'm just looking. He can't stop me from parking in a designated parking space on a public street and reminisce, can he?"

Gooder turned to the guard. "Look, she's right and you know it. She's several yards away from the site. Go on about your business and don't hassle folks."

The man stayed in place, as if daring a confrontation.

"Let's not turn this into a situation, Barry."

Barry glared at them both. Then, muttering words she

preferred not to hear, he strode away. They watched until he reached the site. All the workers turned to look at them. Gooder stood his ground, hands on hips, one resting easily near his weapon until they finally returned to their task. He slipped his sunglasses back on.

"It's a shame what they've done," he said. "Some of the oldest trees in the county, you know."

"Can't have trees in a parking lot, I guess," Jillian didn't try to soften the bitterness in her voice.

"Reckon not." He expelled a deep breath and turned to her. "Listen. You've had a gander at the place, and you've seen what's going on. It's probably best you leave and not come back until the demolition is done. Those are some rough-looking bubbas over there, and—well, I'd hate for something to happen. This town would be mighty boring without you."

She nearly pointed out she was grown and could take care of herself. Gooder too often took on the role of an irritating big brother, and left her feeling at best aggravated and at worst, inept. This time, however, she knew he was right.

"I was getting ready to leave anyway."

He nodded. "I'll wait until you're out of sight."

There. Another example of his "big brother knows best and is taking care of you." Like it or not, it was rather sweet of him, and deep down, she appreciated that he cared.

"See you later, Gooder."

He gave one sharp nod and took a step back. She took one long last look at the treasured old building, then pulled back onto the street, sighing over what had been, what was, and what would be.

Half a block away, on the other side of the street, she spotted a rugged fellow with thick, sandy-blond curls hanging to his shoulders. His beard, a darker blond and generously streaked with gray, reached midway down his red plaid flannel shirt. He stood on the edge of the sidewalk, arms folded, staring at the destruction on the corner.

Jillian slowed as she reached him and called out her open window, "Hi, Gordon!"

He blinked as if she'd startled him, then raised one hand and smiled. Gordon Brett was a kind man, intelligent and highly educated, and while he never rebuffed her friendly approach to him, he never sought out the company of anyone. She pondered stopping to chat with him for a minute or two, but decided it was more important to get back to Bertie and the bakery. She glanced in her rearview mirror after she passed him. He had resumed his sober observation of the corner. Knowing Gordon, he hated the destruction of Guy & Ginger's as much as she did, maybe more. She turned her attention back to the road.

She found her grandmother in the storeroom, moving provisions from one shelf to another. The baking supplies had been in the same place since Jillian could remember, and bakers could find those supplies in the dark, if necessary. The small room smelled of cinnamon, cloves, anise, and lemon.

"What're you doing, Bertie? You practically slap my hands if I move the tin of baking powder two inches."

Bertie whirled around, her face ruddy and damp from work. "There you are! Where have you been? What did you find out? Is it true? Is that big bakery coming to Moss Hollow?"

Jillian reached out to brush away a streak of dust on her grandmother's cheek. The wrinkles had deepened since hearing the rumors, and she hated to see Bertie so worried.

How am I going to take care of this situation? Or worse, what if Bertie's fears are realized and I can't take care of the situation?

She had to give Bertie the news in a calm and confident way, and she needed to do it before Wanda Jean, Maudie, or any other busybody did it for her.

"Let's go sit down for a bit," she said.

Bertie's expression changed from worried to horrified. She clutched her throat. "That's what people say when they're getting ready to tell you about a death or an accident. Spill the bad news right here, right now. Don't make me wait."

"I talked with Megan Farley at the chamber of commerce."

"If anyone would know the truth to any rumors of new businesses in Moss Hollow it would be that gal," Lenora said, joining them. "She didn't come here from the big city to sit around and knit."

"What did she tell you, Jillian?" Bertie's blue-eyed gaze clung to Jillian's face.

Jillian took in a deep breath, steeling herself for her grandmother's reaction. Lenora slipped to Bertie's side and put one arm around her waist.

"It's true, Bertie. There will be a Confections & Donuts franchise on Guy & Ginger's corner."

Lenora staggered a little as Bertie collapsed against her.

"That's it, then," Bertie said. "Unless we can come up with something pretty quick, we're done for." With those words, she sank to the floor, dragging Lenora down with her.

Bertie seldom took time off from The Chocolate Shoppe, but that day Lenora and Jillian persuaded her to leave early.

"Maggie and I have already done most of the cleaning," Lenora said. "It's only an hour until closing time, anyway."

All three women had been sitting on the cement floor of the storeroom for at least fifteen minutes because Bertie seemed disinclined to get up. Maggie, the counter girl, had come in once to see where everyone was, but Lenora dispatched her back to the front.

"Besides," Lenora continued as she huffed and puffed her way to a standing position, "you can't do a blessed thing about a new bakery coming to town. And you ain't doing yourself a lick of good sitting on this hard floor and sighing over the future."

Bertie gave her a sour look.

"She's right," Jillian said. "All you're going to do is make yourself ill and tired, and that won't help The Chocolate Shoppe. I'm not going to let you do that."

"Listen to her. And get yourself up from there."

Jillian stood. She and Lenora stood on either side of Bertie as she got to her feet. Jillian held onto her just in case she started to go down again.

"We're going home and having a nice supper. Then you're going to have a warm bath and turn in early."

"As if I can sleep with this mess going on."

"Then before we go to bed, we're going to watch that Cary Grant and Katharine Hepburn movie you like so much."

"*Bringing Up Baby?*"

"That's the one."

In spite of her anxiety, Bertie's eyes lit up.

"Your dreamboat," Lenora said, nudging Bertie gently with her elbow. "If Cary Grant can't take your mind off your troubles, nobody can."

"Unless it's Gregory Peck."

"Ooh, him too."

"Good." Jillian smiled brightly. "Lenora, you're welcome to join us."

"Thanks, but this is the night I call my daughter and grandbaby."

"We wouldn't want to interfere with that." Bertie patted her friend's arm. "When you talk with her, please tell her I said hello."

"I'll do that."

"And say a prayer for us, will you, honey?" Bertie asked. "I have a lot of faith in your prayers, Lenora."

"I pray for all of us every night, but I'll just pray that much harder tonight."

"Thank you."

"Home sure looks good tonight," Bertie said as they pulled into the driveway. For all its splendor, the Greek revival–style mansion and the manicured front lawn exuded a warm welcome.

"Amen to that," Jillian said.

That relaxed feeling diminished as they entered the fragrant kitchen, and Cornelia turned from the stove. Immediately her face grew pinched and her eyes glittered.

"What's wrong?" Cornelia looked back and forth between them. "Don't try to deny it. I can sense these things, you know."

Jillian figured her great-aunt's "sensing" something was likely because they both came home looking worried.

"Piffle," Bertie muttered.

"What do you mean 'piffle'? It's not piffle." Cornelia followed her to the doorway between the living room and kitchen. "Walk away if you want to, missy, but I can tell when something's up."

"I'm going to go wash my face," Bertie called back.

Cornelia turned and squinted at Jillian, as if Jillian had been up to no good. "I've never known her to go 'wash her face,' as if face-washing is a destination like going to the bank or Acapulco. What's happened?"

"Have you talked with Maudie or Wanda Jean today?" Jillian began to set the table in the adjoining breakfast nook where they took most of their meals.

"I haven't."

Jillian arranged the cutlery carefully in place. "Did anyone call you?"

"Today?"

"Yes."

"Does Raymond count?"

Jillian dropped a fork, and wondered why, after all this time, Cornelia entertained the notion that Jillian might believe her aunt's late husband would call. But there were no reasonable explanations for most of Cornelia Montgomery's bizarre ideas. She conceived them, she believed them, and it was up to the rest of the world to deal with it.

"Uncle Raymond does not count." Jillian took a clean fork from the drawer.

"No one called except that same silly person who calls every day asking for Teresa. No matter that I tell him daily there is no Teresa here, he insists on giving me a spiel."

Jillian sighed. "Aunt Cornelia, his calls come from different phone numbers all over the country. You *know* he's a scammer. Block those calls every time a new number comes up."

"Today the caller ID said it was Children's Cancer Fund, so how am I supposed to know a crook is calling before I answer? It's only after he asks for Teresa that I know it's that same fella. One day last week, the caller ID said State Police Benevolent Society. If the police call, I think I should answer. I don't want to get into trouble with the law."

Jillian suppressed a frustrated sigh.

Cornelia took on a thoughtful expression. "I wonder why he keeps asking for Teresa when I've told him time and again no such person lives here."

A headache had begun at the back of Jillian's head and was working its way around in a tight band. "He's just using that as an opening. He's trying to get money from you—"

"He's not getting one red cent from me. Not one."

"Good. So next time he calls, hang up on him."

"That's ill-mannered."

Jillian groaned deep inside herself. "No, Aunt Cornelia. Scamming people out of their money is ill-mannered. You do not owe him a moment's courtesy, because he wants your bank account number, your credit card number, maybe even your Social Security number. Protecting yourself is vital. The next time you see a number on the caller ID that rouses your suspicions, don't answer."

"You mean just let it ring?"

"That's exactly what I mean. Let them leave a message."

Cornelia turned to open the oven. A blast of heat pushed against them, but she put on oven mitts and headed straight into it.

"So you want me to listen to a ringing telephone all day like it's an angelic choir?" She removed a large rectangular baking pan and set it on a couple of trivets and closed the oven. "I don't care what ringtones you set on that thing, none of them sounds like a choir from heaven."

"If you don't pick up the phone right away, it will stop ringing."

Cornelia's expression said she didn't believe it.

"Do me a favor. Try it next time? Okay?"

Cornelia hesitated, then nodded. "I'll try it, but I don't expect anything to change. Now. Tell me what happened today that has sent my sister off to Wash-My-Face Land."

One never knew how Cornelia would react to bad news. Sometimes she took it in stride and other times she went off the deep end. A quiet but direct response was Jillian's best choice, especially as Bertie wasn't in the room right then, sighing and moaning.

"For Bertie's sake, you need to be calm and reasonable."

"When am I never calm and reasonable?"

Jillian coughed politely into her hand and ignored the question. "We found out this afternoon that Confections & Donuts are coming to Moss Hollow."

Cornelia merely blinked at her and said, "Who?"

"Confections & Donuts."

"Isn't that the little pop music group from Savannah? And why would my sister be upset? She wasn't the least bothered when the Blackwood Brothers came to town that time, back in 1965."

"I'm talking about the company with bakeries all over the United States."

Cornelia frowned in thought, then her face cleared and she snapped her fingers. "Their motto is 'Your family's sweetest friends.' Right?"

"That's the one."

"And they're building a bakery here in town?"

Jillian nodded.

One hand flew to her mouth. "Goodness sakes! So they're the ones—"

"Where Guy & Ginger's used to be."

"And that's why Bertie—"

"Yes, ma'am. She's pretty distressed."

"Of course she is, bless her. She always retreats off to herself when she's upset. Good thing I made her favorite supper."

Jillian hugged her. "Your good food will help her feel better, I'm sure." She pulled back but kept her hands on Cornelia's upper arms and looked into her eyes. "What will do more good than anything else is if we stay peaceful and sensible. If she sees that we're fearful, she'll become even more worried. So let's do our best to keep a positive attitude. Okay?"

Cornelia gently pinched Jillian's cheek. "All righty, honey. We'll be as calm as midnight and sweet as honey cream." She stepped away. "Go ahead and put the broccoli salad on the table. I've got everything ready to dish up."

Jillian took the salad out of the refrigerator and set it on the table. "I'll go see about Bertie."

She hurried to her grandmother's bedroom, the only one located on the main floor, wondering if if those dark, worrisome thoughts had overpowered her. She forced herself to rap on the door rather than fling it wide.

"Bertie?"

The door opened. Bertie was wrapped in a pale-aqua robe, her gray hair covered by a towel. The air was damp and fragrant with lavender.

"I thought you were just going to wash your face."

"I thought so too, but decided to take a nice, refreshing shower instead. I even cracked open that bottle of expensive lavender shower gel you gave me for Christmas."

"Do you mean to tell me today is the first time you've used it?"

Bertie gave her mild smile. "I was saving it."

"For what? A hot date?"

A quick frown chased the smile. "What a way to talk to your own grandmother. A hot date, indeed. No, I was saving it for a time when I needed some extra pampering, like this evening."

"Then you did the right thing. And Aunt Cornelia has made your favorite dinner."

"Chicken pie?"

"The very thing."

"From our grandmother's recipe, I hope."

"I wouldn't doubt it for a minute." Jillian kissed the damp cheek and stepped back. "We're dishing it up right now."

"I'll be there directly."

By the time the chicken pie, fresh corn, buttery mashed potatoes, and Cornelia's bread-and-butter pickles were on the table, Bertie had arrived, still in her robe, but with her damp hair neatly combed and arranged.

"I need to make an appointment for my hair," she said as she sat down. "I'm getting as shaggy as a hippie."

"Wear a hairnet," Cornelia suggested. "No one will notice."

"I wear one when I bake. I'm not wearing one of those things any other time." She passed her gaze over the food. "Cornelia, this meal is exactly what I needed. Let's say grace and dig in."

Cornelia cut into the flaky crust of the chicken pie, steam rising as she dished the serving onto her sister's plate. Bertie wasn't the only one who loved chicken pie. With its tender pieces of plump chicken and savory gravy, the dish was also one of Jillian's favorites.

"How is it, Bertie?" Jillian asked, holding out her plate for a generous serving.

"Mmm," she murmured with her eyes closed. "As good as Mama used to make."

"I knew you'd need it today," Cornelia said. "I felt the bad news coming." Jillian shot her great-aunt a look, warning her to tread lightly, but Cornelia missed it. "Back when we were kids and we were down in the dumps for any reason, Mama's food made the world bearable."

"Right now I don't want to talk about bad news or down-in-the-dumps times or any of that." Bertie's tone was firm, but her voice trembled.

"It's okay, Bertie. Eat and enjoy." Jillian smiled at her. Then she waggled her eyebrows and added, "Remember, we have Cary Grant coming over tonight. Savannah is bringing him." Savannah Cantrell had been Jillian's dearest friend growing up, and they had reestablished their closeness when Jillian moved back to town.

"That's right. Maybe I should dress in something a little less casual."

Jillian giggled. Cornelia looked at the two of them as if they'd lost their minds. "What?"

"Savannah is coming over a little later, and we're going to watch *Bringing Up Baby*."

"I see. Well, if that doesn't make my sister feel young and special again, I don't know what will. I believe she would have named your mother Carrie, if your grandfather had been amenable."

"It's a lovely name," Bertie said primly, "and I'll thank you kindly not to jeer. Please pass the corn."

The rest of the evening passed without further mention of Confections & Donuts. They finished dinner just as Savannah rang the doorbell. The four women moved to the living room, where they enjoyed the movie, chatted pleasantly, and sighed and giggled over Cary Grant's smile and dimpled chin. The twins retired shortly after Savannah left, and Jillian cleaned the kitchen. She had just dried the last dish and put it away when her phone rang.

"Hey Jillian. How are you?" Hunter Greyson asked when she picked up.

Hunter had become a good friend since she'd moved back to Moss Hollow after her life in California came crashing down. He ran Greyson & Sons Funeral Home and also served as the county coroner when needed. They had kissed at the end of a recent date, but she wasn't sure what it had meant, and she hadn't wanted to ask. *That's just not the kind of thing you do*, she thought.

"I'm fine, but it has been a rather distressing day." She turned out the kitchen light and went to settle on the sofa. It was good to hear his voice, and she felt comforted by it.

"Would your distress have anything to do with Confections & Donuts coming to Moss Hollow?"

"Yes. Bertie is really upset."

"I'm sure she is. But I doubt she has as much to worry about as it seems. The Chocolate Shoppe is a favorite around here, and so is everyone who works there. A new bakery might offer a few new things, but I have a strong feeling loyalty will win out."

"I hope you're right."

"I know I am," Hunter said. "I know you're going to be crazy busy for several days, but I wanted to ask you about going with me to a singing at Apple Grove Church on Wednesday night in a couple of weeks. I've been there before, and it's a lot of fun."

"I'd love to go."

They chatted for a few more minutes. Before the call ended, Hunter reminded her to let him know if she or the twins needed anything. She turned off the phone feeling much better than she had all day.

After such a stressful afternoon, the night had been fun and relaxing, and Hunter's phone call had capped off the evening just right. But soon her uneasy feelings crept back in. Jillian feared that the evening had been the calm before the storm.

She was right. The following morning, Bertie didn't get out of bed.

4

There is nothing wrong with me," Bertie snapped at Cornelia and Jillian as they hovered over her. "I'm just malingering a bit today. I have the right to malinger after all these years of hard work."

"Of course you do," Jillian said, patting her hand. Bertie grimaced and yanked free of her grasp.

"Linger all you like, as long as you're not sick," Cornelia said. "If you're sick, I'm calling the doctor."

"*Malinger*, not linger." She waved one hand. "I guess it amounts to the same thing in the long run. At any rate, I'm not sick. Or in pain. I just want to stay here and do some thinking. Jillian, you need to get to the bakery. Tell Lenora I'll be in a bit later. And I do not want her to worry, so don't be dramatic about it. Hear me?"

"Bertie, you know I'm not a dramatic person."

"The way you keep fussing with my blanket and fluffing my pillow, one might think differently. Cornelia, go on about your business. I'll be up soon."

"I'll fetch my tatting and keep you company," she said.

Bertie sat up and glowered at her sister. "No. I want some time to think. That's all. Just leave me alone, both of you."

"Is this about that new bakery coming to town?" Cornelia shook her finger like a mother scolding a child. "Because if it is, Bertie Harper, I have every right to be in on your thinking."

"You may have a right to be in on it, but as the older sister—"

"Older by two minutes!"

"I know what's best for us."

"Oh, forevermore." Cornelia flung out both arms. "All I want is to be here with you in your time of need, and you throw me out into the street."

Bertie huffed.

"Now, Aunt Cornelia," Jillian said firmly, "Bertie has a right to some private time, just like anyone else. There've been times you've closed yourself off from the rest of us."

"Usually because Raymond, Possum, and I needed to communicate." She blinked as if fighting tears. *Crocodile tears*, Jillian thought. "The rest of you jeer at us."

"We don't jeer."

"And I am not throwing you out into the street," Bertie added, "so please never make such an ugly accusation again in this life. Or the next."

Cornelia sniffed and sulked, giving an air of martyrdom.

"Remember what we talked about last night?" Jillian whispered in her ear.

"Yes. All right. Fine." She sniffed again. "I'll be somewhere if you need me. I don't know where exactly, but I'll be there." She sailed out of the room, head high, leading with her chin.

Bertie sighed and lay back. "There are times that woman flat wears me out."

"Don't let her upset you. You know she means well."

"Yes. And if she didn't mean well, I might have thrown her out into the street long before this."

Jillian laughed, and kissed her grandmother's forehead. "You don't mean that and you know it."

"I know I know it. And I know you know I know it. But still . . ." Her face remained sour for a little bit, but then she softened and offered a small smile. "I'm blessed to have both of you, and I know that too. I thank God every day for you, and for my sister. Now." She made a dismissive gesture toward the door. "Get to the bakery, and I'll be along."

"All right. I'll see you later."

Bertie nodded absently, obviously losing herself in her thoughts. As she stepped out the door, Jillian looked back just in time to see her grandmother pull a notebook and pen out from beneath the covers.

Why would she hide paper and pen between the sheets?

On Wednesday morning, four unfamiliar women settled at a corner table in the bakery. They got treats and coffee, then put their heads together as if they were planning something secretive and important. A steady stream of regular customers came and went, and by the time an hour had passed, it was business as usual at The Chocolate Shoppe. But the women stayed in the corner.

Bertie, who continued to be quieter and more thoughtful than was customary, kept glancing toward the corner.

"Something interesting about those ladies?" Jillian finally asked her.

Bertie polished the same clean spot on the counter, never taking her eyes off the women. "Look at them. They've only taken a bite or two of each thing they've ordered. They never finish it, but order something else." She glanced at Jillian. "When Stewie Franks came in and saw them in his corner, he stood dead still in the middle of the room. I thought for a minute he was going to take his order to go, bless his heart."

"Well, he has sat at that table every morning for years."

"Our regular customers know it's Stewie's, but those new ones don't. I'm glad he finally settled at another table. If he didn't get to read the Atlanta paper every day, he'd feel adrift. He's why I subscribe." They looked at the elderly white-haired man who was still reading the paper, sipping his coffee. He was happy and relaxed, his hearing aid on the table. He always said he liked to read the paper in peace.

Bertie fixed her attention on the women again. "Do you know those gals, Jillian?"

"I've never seen them before."

Bertie leaned closer. "I know what they're doing."

"Besides visiting?"

"They're corporate spies."

Jillian raised both eyebrows. "Do you have any baking secrets they're after?"

Bertie scowled at her. "Baking secrets?"

"That's what corporate spies do. They steal your secrets, plans, and formulas, and then they use them for their own profit." She dipped her head toward the group in the corner. "I doubt they're spying. I think they're evaluating the baked goods."

"Whatever it is they're up to, I'm sure it all has to do with that new bakery."

"Maybe. Maybe not. Would you like me to go ask them?" She fervently hoped Bertie wouldn't take her up on this offer.

"Looks like you won't have to. They're leaving, and look—they brought their own to-go containers."

The quartet of women had put all their partially nibbled leftovers in small plastic containers with lids. They walked out of the bakery without making eye contact or speaking to anyone.

"Shall I go after them, Bertie?" *Why am I offering to do silly things I don't want to do?*

Bertie stared down at the place on the counter she continued to wipe. She said nothing for a bit. "No. If they're up to no good, this isn't the last we've seen or heard of them."

Up to no good? Jillian hoped all this quiet contemplation didn't mean her grandmother was slipping into a version of paranoia. On the other hand, she had to admit the group's behavior was peculiar.

Stewie folded the paper and put his hearing aid back in his ear. "Hey, Bertie. You reckon The Chocolate Shoppe will still be up and running after Confections & Donuts gets to town?"

Bertie gave him a long look, then turned and went into the back. Lenora was clearing the mess the four women had left behind. She parked a fist on each hip and scowled at the old man.

"Stewie Franks, you come into this bakery every blessed day, and you hardly ever say a word. Why on God's green earth did you pick today to talk, and why would you say something like that?"

His bushy white brows went up. "What? Why're you so mad? I was just asking what everyone else has been thinking and saying behind her back." He pointed in the direction Bertie had taken. "She'd better come up with some answers, 'cause I'm not the only one who wants to know."

"We'd all like to know," said a woman filling her cup at the coffee station. Nearly everyone else in the bakery agreed.

"Listen," Jillian said, "no one is sure exactly what's going to happen, but I do know one thing—my grandmother's bakery has been the best in the area for many years and will continue to be the best. You love the baked goods here at The Chocolate Shoppe, right?"

A chorus of approval went up.

"Good. The quality of food here is not going to change, no matter who comes to town. You can count on that."

"But y'all don't serve divinity," Matt Harris said, "or caramels, or fudge. People who like fresh candy can't get it anywhere in town unless they make it at home. I've seen the commercials for Confections & Donuts. They have all kinds of candies."

"You don't need candy," his wife said. "I've already let out your britches as far as they'll go."

Everyone laughed.

"She's right," Matt said with a grin. He looked past Jillian to Bertie who had returned to the front and stood behind the counter, listening to the exchange. "Still and all, Bertie, the new place is going to offer a lot more than this little place can."

"You're gonna have to step lively to keep up, I'm thinkin', and you ain't exactly a spring chicken," Stewie said. "I should know. You got a couple of years on me."

All eyes were on Bertie and the atmosphere in the bakery soured. She came around the counter to face everyone.

"I don't have a crystal ball to see into the future, so I can't give you the definitive answer you want. All I can say is you have been my neighbors and friends for many years now, and I hope you'll continue to be my customers." She passed a look around, meeting every gaze. "But I guess that will be up to you, won't it?"

Complete silence fell. Bertie went to the coffee station, grabbed both pots and turned. "Okay, who wants regular and who wants decaf?"

With that, the silence cracked, but the uneasy feeling lingered, even after the shop closed that afternoon, and Jillian and Bertie returned to Belle Haven.

At the supper table, Cornelia chattered a mile a minute, doing her best to draw Bertie out of her quiet, pensive mood. At last, she put down her fork, folded her hands in her lap and stared at her sister.

"Just in case you've been wondering, I've forgiven you for throwing me out of your room this morning."

Bertie stared at her, as if something about Cornelia's features needed to be adjusted or memorized.

The front doorbell rang, but the two women seemed oblivious to it. Jillian went to answer. She grabbed the arm of the smiling dark-haired woman outside and pulled her across the threshold.

"Am I glad to see you, Savannah!"

"Uh-oh. Whenever I hear that, I know there's a problem."

"You could say that."

Savannah lost her smile. "Is Bertie upset again?"

"People were talking in the bakery. Speculating on when we'd go out of business and so forth."

"People and their talk."

"Exactly. Come on into the kitchen. We're still at the supper table."

They stepped into the kitchen, where the twins greeted Savannah.

"Hello, dear, how are you?" Bertie asked.

"Have a seat, honey." Cornelia got up. "Have you eaten? I'll go get another plate. How about some ice cream?"

Savannah held up one hand. "I've eaten, thanks. And no sweets after six p.m. That's my new rule."

"That's a terrible rule," Bertie said, sighing.

"Except for sweet tea, right?" Cornelia set a glass in front on her.

"Thank you. I won't turn that down." She sipped. "So what's going on?"

Before any of them could respond, someone knocked on the back veranda door.

"Who on earth would be calling on us back there?" Cornelia's face creased as she looked in the direction of the living room.

"Sit down, Aunt Cornelia." Jillian stood. "I'll see who it is and what they want."

When she saw the bearded man standing at the glass door, she halted for a few seconds. It wasn't that she was unwilling to open the door to Gordon Brett, but rather because he had never called on them before. In fact, she was pretty sure Gordon never called on anyone.

She opened the door, smiling at him. "Good evening, Gordon. Come on in."

"Thank you, Jillian." He paused to make good use of the doormat before stepping inside. He held a large manila envelope in one hand. "I hope you don't mind me dropping by like this. I cut across the way." He pointed toward the stand of trees beyond the back garden. He lived across the meadow and through the woods behind the mansion on the estate he'd inherited from his grandfather. "It's shorter."

"We don't mind you dropping by at all. It's nice to see you."

He glanced around the shining-clean living room with its mixture of beautiful antiques and comfortable modern furniture. "This is a lovely home."

"Thanks. It's been in the family for a long time."

He smiled. "Mine too, as you know. Pappaw's place was always nice, but nothing compared to Belle Haven."

When he moved back to the area a few years ago, everyone had hoped he'd restore the long-neglected place. The original home had been destroyed on Sherman's March through Georgia during the Civil War, but Gordon's ancestors had built a smaller house to replace it in 1870. It was another landmark that time had touched with ungentle hands. Gordon had done some restoration work, but in his own way, which was nothing like his neighbors had anticipated. Rather than the expected conventional manicured lawns and shrubs, he'd turned the four acres around the house into gardens for produce. The house looked shabby with its peeling paint and sagging porch. Jillian was unsure if Gordon had ever had the electricity reconnected.

"We're in the kitchen at the supper table. Won't you join us?"

He looked uncomfortable. "I don't want to intrude."

"You aren't intruding. Have you had dinner?"

"I've already eaten, thank you." He followed her to the kitchen, but hesitated when he saw the others. "I'm sorry. I can come back later."

"Nonsense," Cornelia said. "Come and sit down. Have you had your supper?"

"Yes, ma'am. Thank you." He nodded a greeting to everyone and sat down next to Jillian, across from Savannah.

"How are you, Gordon?" Savannah smiled at him. She had looks and personality that caused men of all sizes, shapes, and ages to sit up and take notice. Gordon returned her smile with an appreciative light in his eyes, but nothing more.

"Just fine, Miss Cantrell, thank you."

Cornelia set a glass of tea in front of him, and resumed her place at the table. "What brings you to Belle Haven? I don't believe you've ever been here."

"No, ma'am, I haven't. I'm not much for socializing, although I don't mind being in the presence of charming ladies from time to time."

"Listen to him," Cornelia said, batting her lashes as if she were seventeen.

Bertie frowned at her. "For heaven's sake, Cornelia."

"I'm just being friendly."

Gordon shifted in his seat and cleared his throat. "As I said, I'm not much of one for socializing. And I don't generally beat around the bush, so I'll get to the point of my visit."

"Please do." Bertie gave him a stiff little smile, almost as if she was so lost in her worry over the bakery that she was hardly aware of his presence.

"I'm sure you know by now what has happened at the corner lot across from the high school."

"We certainly do," Jillian said.

"Bertie has talked of little else for the last two days." Cornelia laid a hand on her sister's arm. "No, that's not quite true. Bertie has talked very little, period. But it's weighing on her mind."

He looked at Bertie who nodded. "It sits like a stone in my thoughts," she said. "I'm sick with worry about what that new business will mean for The Chocolate Shoppe."

"It lingers in my mind too. Not for the same reason as yours, Miss Bertie, although I share your concern for your business. For all the small businesses in Moss Hollow, in fact. If Confections & Donuts is allowed to build here, it will open the door to other such businesses. Box stores, chain stores, franchises, fast-food drive-throughs, huge discount stores. If that happens, our town will forever be changed."

"That's exactly what Megan Farley told me," Jillian said. "Only she thinks that's a good thing."

His face darkened. "Megan Farley is a menace to this town. She wants it to change, to turn into something it's never been—a commercial center."

"That's why she was brought here from Atlanta and put in as head of the chamber of commerce," Savannah said. "She's a mover and a shaker, and she's business-oriented."

Cornelia shifted in her chair, a frown between her eyebrows. "That doesn't make a lot of sense to me. The chamber is made up of Moss Hollow business owners, and all of them are small business people. Not a corporate CEO among them. So why do they want someone like Megan?"

"I have a feeling it was her reputation that caught their eye," Jillian said, "but I'm confident they intended that energy to go toward helping existing businesses do better, not bring in big competition to wipe them out."

"So you agree with me." Bertie's face was drawn, her eyes frightened. Jillian hadn't meant to upset her grandmother further.

While she sought words to smooth her gaffe, Gordon spoke.

"I'm a man who enjoys the natural world, not the man-made one, as you probably know. That's why I left my professorial position at the university. I'm unsure why I ever thought I was suited to teaching computer science." His glance went around the table. "I don't like wanton destruction of nature to make room for more parking lots or new housing divisions. There is enough shelter and opportunity for everyone if we use what's already here." He leaned forward. "Mankind is destroying the planet by constantly building something new, something bigger, something that they think is better. Urban sprawl has to stop."

"Amen!" Bertie slapped the flat of her hand against the tabletop.

Jillian tried to interject a note of hope. "Moss Hollow is a long way from reaching urban sprawl."

"But it has started," Gordon said. "You saw what they did to those trees at Guy & Ginger's."

"What did they do?" Cornelia's eyes were wide. "Tell me no one cut them down."

"They bulldozed them out of the ground and cut them up." Gordon paused for dramatic effect. "And today they took down the building."

There was a brief, thick silence.

"Mercy." Bertie hid her face in her hands. Cornelia looked as if she might be sick.

"Mercy is not what these people are all about," Gordon said. "And they have to be stopped."

"But what can we do?" Savannah asked.

Gordon held up the manila envelope. "I have written two petitions. One demands a cessation of all work on the corner of Maple and Catalpa—that is, the new bakery. The second is to block further big businesses from developing Moss Hollow. Will you sign?"

Bertie sat up. "Hand them over, Gordon. Do you have a pen?"

While Bertie signed, Jillian and Savannah exchanged glances. It seemed unlikely a petition would have enough power to halt construction of the new bakery, no matter how many signed it. Jillian doubted anything could block new businesses from coming to town. While she agreed in principle with Gordon, she also recognized the wave of the future. That wave would swallow them all, sooner or later.

The following Saturday, in the wee hours of the morning, sirens piercing the darkness awoke the people in and around Moss Hollow. When Jillian looked out her window, the sky in the distance over the village glowed orange.

Cornelia emerged from her room at the same time Jillian came out of her own. "Did you hear them too, honey?" Cornelia tightened the sash of her lavender robe about her thin waist.

"I did. Something is burning in town."

"Lawsy, what next?"

They hurried downstairs and found Bertie on the front steps, looking toward Moss Hollow. The glowing sky caused the hairs on the nape of Jillian's neck to stand up.

"Could that be The Chocolate Shoppe on fire?" Cornelia asked, staring at the sky.

"Oh no." Bertie gasped and swayed. Jillian grabbed her. "Lenora!"

Grateful that she'd had the foresight to grab it, Jillian snatched her cell phone from the pocket of her robe and called Lenora's phone number. Waiting for her to answer, she beckoned both women.

"Come back inside, both of you. Bertie, you are barefooted. Come on."

"But I have to know!"

Jillian prayed for Lenora's well-being and hoped her grandmother's business was safe and whole. "If you'll come inside and put on your slippers, I'll drive to the bakery and check on everything. Okay?"

"Would you, please, honey?"

"Of course." She led Bertie into the house, and looked over her head at Cornelia. "Would you make some of that chamomile tea I bought the other day?"

Why isn't Lenora answering her phone?

"Sure, sweetheart. Now, sister, you settle down right here." She grabbed Bertie's hand and pulled her toward an armchair while Jillian got the soft house slippers Bertie kept under her bed.

"Put these on. I won't be long."

"Take your phone."

"I have it." *And all I get from Lenora's phone is voice mail.*

A cold knot clenched her stomach as she fumbled with the keys to start the car, even as she tried Lenora's phone again.

"Pick up the phone, Lenora. Please, please, please!"

Still not raising Lenora, Jillian called Hunter, praying that she wouldn't awaken him.

"Hello, Jillian."

"You're up!"

"Oliver called me and said I probably should come down to the funeral home." Oliver Kent was Hunter's assistant at the mortuary. "I don't think we're in danger from the fire, so I'm heading back to the house. What are you doing?"

"I'm headed to town to check on The Chocolate Shoppe," Jillian said. "I'm worried because I can't get Lenora on the phone."

"I'm turning around," Hunter said without hesitation. "I'll meet you at the bakery as soon as I can." He signed off to allow Jillian to keep calling Lenora.

At two-thirty in the morning, traffic going into town was heavier than she'd seen during the lunch hour on any given Monday. Smoke dimmed the clear night air and the acrid odor grew strong the nearer she got to the city limits. Jillian soon realized the fire was on the far side of town. The Chocolate Shoppe and Lenora were well out of its path. Relief flowed through her so strongly she could hardly feel the steering wheel in her hands.

Reaching the bakery, she recognized Hunter's car in one of the streetside parking spaces. He was standing beside it, and raised his arm in recognition. Jillian motioned toward the alley leading to the employee parking lot at the back. By the time she had parked, Hunter was beside her, an expression of concern shrouding his face.

Lenora's car was in its usual place, and a light gleamed from an upper window. But if Lenora was up, why wasn't she answering her telephone?

Jillian unlocked the back door, and she and Hunter stepped into the bakery. They moved toward the stairs. "Lenora?" she called.

No response.

"It's Jillian and Hunter. We're coming up."

The steps to the apartment creaked beneath their steps as they ascended. The landing was dark, except for a small night-light in an outlet near the door. She knocked, but the door never opened.

"Lenora!" She knocked again, louder. When the door remained closed, she turned the knob. Locked.

Surely she couldn't have slept through the sirens, her ringing telephone, and Jillian pounding on her door, yelling.

"What should I do?" she asked Hunter.

"Do you want me to break it down?"

"No. Let me try again.

She rattled and pulled the knob, then twisted and pushed. She swallowed hard and did her best to control panic, but her mind's eye conjured the image of Lenora lying unconscious or worse on the floor of the apartment. She was about to take Hunter up on his offer when the back door rattled, the sound of a key scraped, and the back door of the bakery opened below them.

She strained her ears and heard a familiar voice quietly singing, almost whispering, a hymn. Lenora almost reached the top step before she spotted Jillian and Hunter on the landing at her apartment door. She gasped and staggered, barely catching hold of the rail to keep her balance.

"Good gracious! Jillian Green, what are you doing skulking around my apartment at this hour? And Hunter . . . Is that you?"

Jillian gaped at her. "I thought something had happened to you. Your car is here and your light is on, but you didn't answer your phone or my knocking." She paused to gulp in a breath.

"I went with Hattie Florence Freeman to see the fire. What're you doing here?"

"The sirens woke us up. You can see the light of the fire from Belle Haven. We were worried about you, so I came to see if you were all right."

"I'm fine, as you can see."

In the dim light, Jillian ran her gaze down Lenora, noted the hem of her nightgown beneath the raincoat she wore over it, and below, her flat-soled chenille slippers. Jillian herself was in blue-and-white striped pajamas and a robe that had seen better days ten years ago. She was surprised to notice she was wearing two different sneakers.

"Before you ask, I'll tell you. The sirens woke me up too. I heard fire trucks and ambulances and volunteer folks driving in from all over. Then Hattie Florence called. She was beside herself. She has a heart condition, and I didn't want her to keel over, so when she asked me to go with her to see what was going on, I went."

"And?" Hunter broke in.

"And there's nary a thing left on Guy & Ginger's lot. All those building supplies for the new bakery? Burnt to a crisp. And it looks like the shoe store next to it caught fire too."

"No wonder we could see it from Belle Haven."

"It's quite a blaze. Fire departments from every town in Nathan County are there. They were hosing down the furniture store when we left to make sure it didn't catch. We didn't linger because the last thing firefighters need are a bunch of rubbernecks. But you know how people's curiosity gets up over something like this."

"Then I'd better not go over there and add to the commotion," Jillian said.

"Good thinking. I always said you were a smart girl." Lenora fished her keys out of her pocket and crossed to her door. "What about you, Hunter?"

"I've already been. Made sure everything was all right at the funeral home and left it in Oliver's capable hands and started back home. That's when Jillian called."

"And you came to make sure she was all right." Lenora glanced at Jillian. "You'd better not let this one get away, honey. He's a keeper."

Jillian blushed and ducked her head, wondering how Hunter was reacting to Lenora's assertion.

"Well, do you two wanna come in?"

"No," Jillian said. "Bertie and Cornelia are probably in full panic mode by now. And I've kept Hunter out way past his bedtime." She smiled at the handsome man beside her, hoping her little joke had broken the awkwardness of the moment.

Lenora unlocked her apartment door and opened it. Light spilled out of her small sitting room and onto the landing. She turned to Jillian. "I'm worried about your grandma. She's taking the news of that new bakery mighty hard."

"I know. It's not like her to let something get to her like this. I think she's starting to feel beaten." Jillian thought for a moment. "Of course, there's no telling what this fire might mean. Maybe they'll decide not to go through with their plans."

"Best cure for Bertie is to make sure she feels necessary, irreplaceable to the bakery and to Moss Hollow. I'm all for her taking a break when she needs one, but I'm afraid she might want to start staying home all the time."

"That would be disastrous on so many levels."

"Amen, sister. So let's make sure that doesn't happen. Deal?"

"Absolutely deal! See you tomorrow, Lenora," she said. "Get some rest."

"'Bye, honey. Thanks for checking up on me. You scared ten years off my life, but I'll get over it."

When Jillian got back to Belle Haven, the sitting room and kitchen were empty. She found Bertie and Cornelia in Bertie's bed, propped up on fat pillows, each clutching a glass of milk. In that moment, she saw past the years that had aged them, and caught a glimpse of two young girls who always turned to each other for comfort.

"Lenora called," Bertie said.

"Did she?"

"She said you and Hunter scared her witless."

Jillian gave a small laugh. "We did, but I think she's okay now."

"When did you pick up Hunter?"

"I didn't pick up Hunter, Bertie. He came to The Chocolate Shoppe because he thought I might need help finding Lenora."

"Well wasn't that just about the sweetest thing a man could ever do?" Cornelia gulped the last of her milk. "Helping our damsel in distress."

"I wasn't in distress." Jillian sat on the edge of the bed and took Cornelia's empty glass. "Well, maybe I was a little in distress. He just wanted to make sure Lenora was all right."

"Sure. You just keep thinking that," Cornelia said, giving her a knowing look.

Jillian decided to change the subject. "Anyway, The Chocolate Shoppe isn't in any danger from the fire, so we can all get some sleep."

"That might not mean anything," Cornelia said cryptically.

Bertie handed her half-full glass to Jillian. "I never did like warm milk, even when Cornelia doctors it."

"You love cinnamon and honey in everything else. You're too picky, Bertie."

"I'm not picky, but I know what I don't like. Hiding it behind spices and sweetness won't change a blessed thing."

The last thing Jillian wanted to hear that night—besides more sirens—was her great-aunt and grandmother bickering.

"Aunt Cornelia, what did you mean when you said 'that might not mean anything'?"

Cornelia blinked at Jillian as if her words were not computing, so Jillian continued. "A minute ago I said the fire isn't threatening the bakery and you said 'that might not mean anything.'"

"She meant maybe someone set that fire on purpose," Bertie said.

"That's right." Cornelia nodded vigorously. "No one is happy about Guy & Ginger's being bulldozed, so maybe someone decided to get even."

"Even if that's the case, it would have been an act against that company. It has nothing to do with our bakery. I don't think anyone in town would want to burn down The Chocolate Shoppe."

The twins looked at each other.

"She has a point," Bertie said.

Cornelia nodded. "A good point. Our Jillian is a smart girl."

"Feeling better now?" Jillian asked.

"How can we feel better if someone is going around burning down the town?" Cornelia countered.

A great weariness crept over Jillian, reminding her that she'd been wakened far too early and done far too much for that hour of the morning.

"Aunt Cornelia, please don't borrow trouble."

"I'm not borrowing anything, but kindly remember our gentleman caller at supper the other night."

"Gordon Brett? What about him?"

"Do you recall what he said?"

"I remember, and he made some very good points."

The twins looked at each other again, before Bertie spoke. "Do you think it's coincidental that he talked about putting a stop to new businesses, then a new business burns down?"

"You think there is a connection between Gordon and the fire?"

The two women stared at her, and she was again struck by their childlike vulnerability. They nodded in perfect timing with each other.

"He said he wanted it stopped, that something had to be done," Cornelia said, leaning forward. "You heard him."

They had a point, and she knew it. Looking at them, their faces pale, their eyes wide, she knew the last thing either of them needed was more anxiety.

"Gordon Brett is an educated man—"

"And so was that fellow a few years ago," Cornelia said. "You know. The Unicyclist."

"Who?"

"The Unicyclist. You remember. They had this sketch of him all over the news, although what good that did, I don't know. Sunglasses, hooded sweatshirt. He could've been anyone."

"You mean the Unabomber?"

"That's what I said."

"No, Cornelia, you did not," Bertie said. "You called him the 'Unicyclist.' That's someone who rides a one-wheeled cycle."

Cornelia rolled her eyes and waved one hand. "Jillian knew what I meant. And my point, which was, of course, that he was a very educated man but he turned out to be a certified nutcase."

"That's true." Bertie looked at Jillian. "Living all alone, scroungy and strange."

"Listen, you two. Gordon lives by himself, and he's a little eccentric, but just because someone chooses to do without modern conveniences and necessities does not mean they are insane. Or criminal."

Cornelia leaned back against the pillows and sighed. "I have to admit, he isn't scroungy." A dreamy look crossed her face. "In fact, despite that woolly beard, he was quite charming."

"Heaven help us!" Bertie glared at her sister. "Just because he flirted with you—"

"You think he did?" Cornelia asked eagerly.

Bertie scoffed. "Look at you, old enough to be his grandmother.

A few minutes ago you were ready to sic the police on him."

"Aunt Cornelia. Bertie. Please stop fussing. You need your rest, and for that matter, so do I. Would you *please* put all of this out of your mind and get some sleep?"

Bertie turned a sharp look on her. "Are you feeling okay, honey?"

Jillian stopped rubbing her temple and straightened her spine.

"Are you sick?" Cornelia leaned forward again, reaching out with one hand as if about to lay a palm against a feverish brow.

"I'm fine. Just tired."

"Then you need to go to bed." Bertie's tone and expression indicated that Jillian had chosen to sit up late because she had nothing better to do.

"I can't sleep if I know you two are in here bickering and coming up with stories to upset each other."

"If we promise to stop talking and lie here quietly, will you go to bed?"

She nodded.

"Then that's what we'll do." Bertie rearranged her pillows and snuggled down. "Cornelia, turn off the lamp."

Jillian got up. "Wait a second." She kissed both wrinkled foreheads, tucked the blankets around them, and smiled. "Get some rest, you two. And don't make me come back in here." Bertie started to protest, but Jillian raised a hand to cut her off. "Hey, I'm just repeating what you told me when I stayed with you overnight as a little girl."

"We'll be good," Cornelia said in mock seriousness.

"Goodnight, then."

"'Night."

As she headed upstairs to her own room, Jillian thought about all that had happened before the day had even begun. Bertie and Cornelia. Lenora. And Hunter. *He did come to my rescue, didn't he?* Jumbled thoughts raced through Jillian's head like a wildfire.

What would I do without these people in my life? I hope nothing ever comes between us.

6

"It's a shame House's Shoe Emporium and Rodger's Furniture Mart got caught in that fire," Maudie said Sunday afternoon at the meeting of the Southern Sweetie Pies. The group of friends and baking enthusiasts met each week after church at The Chocolate Shoppe.

"At least the furniture store didn't burn," Annalise Reed said. Annalise, whose husband was vice president at the bank in Moss Hollow, was an ardent social volunteer in town.

"But I'm sure their inventory got soaked," Lenora said.

Jillian nodded. "I suppose it will be awhile before we know how the fire started."

"They're looking over the site today," said Laura Lee Zane, one of the deputies with the sheriff's department.

Bertie's forehead creased. "Who are 'they'?"

"The sheriff and the fire chief."

"Aha!" Wanda Jean Maplewood nearly stood in triumph. Everyone looked at her. "So it *is* suspicious. I told you, Maudie. I said that fire didn't start itself."

"You don't need to sound so happy about being right." Lenora scowled at her. "The Houses and the Rodgers have lost their businesses, or as good as."

Some grumbling ensued, and Laura Lee held up one hand to get the women's attention.

"Every fire has to be investigated, so that doesn't mean it's arson. Insurance companies have to know how the fire started, the amount of damage that's been done, and so forth. So I would say you shouldn't assume this fire was deliberately set.

There will be a report issued when the investigation is over."

A brief silence fell before Cornelia spoke up. "Well, with you being a deputy and all, I reckon you should know. At least it slowed down Confections & Donuts."

"It might have slowed them down," Bertie replied, "but I'll bet it hasn't stopped them."

Bertie wasn't the only one who felt that way. The topic of Confections & Donuts was on everyone's tongue and had dominated most of the conversations at The Chocolate Shoppe the previous week. Jillian did her best to distract Bertie from the various speculations and remarks customers unthinkingly uttered. Lenora encouraged Bertie to spend most of her time in the kitchen and concocted as many baking disasters as possible to keep her there.

That won't work forever. What are we going to do?

Monday evening, surly faced Sheriff Coy Henderson showed up at Belle Haven. Stocky with iron-gray hair and a no-nonsense demeanor, Henderson was a man who left the impression that he would get the job done, whatever it was, and all by himself, if necessary. The women of Belle Haven greeted him with warm hospitality and plied him with hot coffee and cherry pie.

As usual, the sheriff was short on small talk and long on terseness.

"What do you know about Gordon Brett?" he asked as Cornelia seated him in the breakfast nook just off the kitchen.

"Not much. Why?" Bertie stood in the kitchen doorway and dried her hands on a dish towel.

"He's polite as all get-out, but he's an odd duck," Cornelia added as she poured him a cup of coffee.

Henderson looked at Jillian and lifted one eyebrow.

"He's a neighbor," she said. "A nice guy."

"An odd duck?"

Cornelia huffed. "That's what I just said. Coy Henderson, do you need new batteries for your hearing aid?"

He glanced at her and shook his head, then turned a silent, inquiring look to Jillian.

"He's . . . different."

Henderson kept his steely eyed gaze pinned on her, waiting for more.

"He's smart, well-spoken."

"Charming," Cornelia said softly. She placed a slice of pie in front of the sheriff.

"Cornelia, do you mind?" Bertie gave her an exasperated look. "He's mannerly, Coy. And a bit flattering, which my sister took as serious."

"You never get too old to be told you're beautiful," Cornelia said with a sniff.

"He did not say one word about anyone being beautiful."

"He called us charming ladies, and that's the same thing."

"How can you be so silly?"

Sheriff Henderson ignored the bickering. "When's the last time you saw Gordon?"

"He was here just a few days ago. Why do you ask?" Bertie put one hand to her throat. "Has something happened to him?"

"Did he say or do anything to arouse your suspicions? Other than being an 'odd duck,' that is?"

"He wanted us to sign a paper," Cornelia announced.

"A paper?"

"A couple of petitions," Jillian said. "One to stop Confections

& Donuts from building, and another to halt any other large company from coming into Moss Hollow." She had a feeling he already knew about the petitions.

"While he was here, did he give any indication that he was going to take further steps to stop the new bakery?"

"You mean like setting fire to it?" Jillian asked mildly. The sheriff merely held Jillian's gaze. "No. He said nothing about destruction of property."

Henderson turned his speculative gaze to Bertie and Cornelia. "Anything you need to tell me?"

They blinked at him wordlessly. Cornelia pointed to the pie he had yet to taste. "You want some ice cream on that?"

The Sunday afternoon before the scheduled opening of Confections & Donuts, the Sweetie Pies talked of nothing else at The Chocolate Shoppe. Most of their recent meetings had been heavily laced with speculation about the new bakery and updates as to the fast-moving progress of the building.

"I fail to understand why they thought it necessary to keep the company name a secret from us," Savannah said. "If word hadn't leaked out, we probably wouldn't know a thing about it until the doors open this Tuesday."

"You can thank Rod Douglas at the newspaper for that," Annalise said.

"It wouldn't have made it into the paper if it wasn't for Maudie," Wanda Jean said.

"What I'd like to know is how Maudie found out when the entire town seemed clueless?"

All eyes turned to Maudie. Her short, snow-white hair gleamed like a beacon in the room. "I have my ways," she said, clearly enjoying being the only one in the know.

"Peeking in windows and listening in doorways, I suspect," Lenora said. "Ever since Nathan County got rid of party lines, Maudie Honeycutt hasn't heard nearly enough juicy gossip."

That brought a burst of laughter, but Maudie seemed oblivious to it.

"I can't help it if I have a nose for news and sharp hearing. Besides, people like to be informed."

"That's right!" Wanda Jean's face was pink. Her eyes flashed. "There's no reason to pick on Maudie."

"So tell us, Maudie," Cornelia said, "who started that fire?"

"I have no idea."

"I'm sure you must have suspicions."

She and Wanda Jean exchanged glances. "I don't want to spread unfounded rumors."

"Since when?" Annalise hooted.

"I wish Laura Lee didn't have to work today," Cornelia said. "Maybe she knows something by now."

"Even if she did, she couldn't tell us," Wanda Jean said. She looked at the others. "We asked her last week and the week before and the week before that. Her answer has been the same."

"Because she's hiding something." Maudie tapped the side of her nose as if she were in on a secret.

"No, it isn't. It's because she's a law enforcement officer and good at her job," Jillian said. "Besides, didn't you read the official report in the newspaper?"

"It's my considered opinion that law enforcement knows a lot more than they are letting on," Wanda Jean said. "Even when it's a matter of public record."

Savannah gave the woman a look of strained patience. "If

that's the case, and there's more information to be gained, then anyone can go look at that record. And lay rumors to rest."

"Y'all are making me tired." Bertie got to her feet. "Let's call it a day. I'm going home. Jillian, you lock up. Cornelia, you coming?"

"Right behind you, sister."

The women of the meeting looked at one another, murmuring and muttering as they left the bakery.

"Jillian, tell your granny to take a chill pill," Wanda Jean said. "In fact, tell her to take two." She stalked out of The Chocolate Shoppe in a huff, Maudie behind her.

"Good gravy," Savannah said as Jillian locked the door.

"Good gravy for sure." Lenora started gathering used cups and paper plates from the tables. "That new place is causing trouble in more ways than one." She threw everything in the trash, then turned and folded her arms. A huge frown puckered her features.

"Now what's that look about?" Jillian asked.

"Way I hear it, most folks in town are happy to be getting another bakery. A big one at that. Makes us look more urban, someone said to me the other day. Right in front of your grandma. She carried those words around with her all day."

Jillian winced. "I have heard a lot both ways about Confections & Donuts, although I have to admit, I have heard way more pros."

"Me too. And no one seems to think twice about bringing their opinions right into this bakery and sharing them. How can people be so insensitive?"

"You think Bertie will lose business?"

Lenora hesitated, then nodded. "Girls, we gotta do all we can to make sure The Chocolate Shoppe doesn't fail. And that means we fight the blues and the fear. We gotta do it for Bertie's sake, if nothing else."

Lenora's words rang in Jillian's mind as she drove across town to witness the ribbon-cutting ceremony two days later. Bertie insisted she go and take pictures.

"Take notes too. Listen to what people are saying, then I want you to tell me every detail."

Every detail, Jillian repeated silently. She had no intention of sharing any worrisome details with Bertie and Cornelia.

No expense had been spared for the opening of Confections & Donuts. The building had been erected in record time following the fire. Now a huge pink balloon tethered in the parking lot swayed gracefully in the breeze. As a beacon for the grand opening, it was big enough and high enough that it could be seen from nearly anywhere in town.

Available parking near the bakery was nonexistent. Judging by the number of cars, she wondered if that day had been deemed a local holiday because no one seemed to be at work. She sought and found a spot a few streets away and walked to her destination. Country music wailed through loud speakers. In the parking lot, pink and white flags and streamers fluttered. Children had pink balloons and party hats. Several trim young women in pink dresses and ruffled white pinafores carried trays filled with free pastries or cups of coffee. Eager onlookers accepted them.

A huge pink-and-white–checked ribbon stretched across the doorway. Jillian spotted Megan Farley chatting with the mayor near the door, an oversize pair of scissors in her hand. The local radio station's van was parked close to the corner of the bakery, set up for a remote broadcast from the grand opening. A man was interviewing a tall redhead in a petal-pink suit and matching high heels.

"Have one of our free, fresh, and famous doughnuts?" A beaming girl held a piled-high tray out to Jillian. The doughnuts were plump, with icing that glistened in the sunshine and a slight almond scent rising from them. Were these pastries part of the instrument that would destroy her grandmother's livelihood? As tantalizing as they looked and smelled, Jillian's stomach turned at the sight.

She forced herself to smile. "No thanks."

The waitress looked surprised. "You sure?" She held the tray closer to Jillian, as if proximity would break down her resistance. "They're the best you'll find anywhere."

"I rather doubt it," Jillian said, backing away.

"It's true, and they're free today. If you go across town, you have to pay for a smaller doughnut of inferior quality."

"No thank you." She turned and walked away, jaw clenched to keep furious words from spewing. She threaded her way through the crowd to the new building with its pink stucco walls and peeked into one of the huge shining plate-glass windows. Inside she saw pink and white floor tiles, white bistro tables and booths with pink cushions, and wallpaper that looked like pink gingham.

"Mercy me," she whispered and took a quick photo through the glass to show Bertie and Cornelia. Bertie had told her to get lots of pictures, but looking at the throng of customers, the presence of the city officials, and the radio station's van, Jillian slipped her phone back into her purse. There was no reason to show her grandmother and great-aunt the abundance of customers and lavish publicity.

Her gaze swept the crowd, spotting more familiar faces than she could count at a glance. Wanda Jean and Maudie gleefully consumed doughnuts, looking around, then bending their heads close together to talk as if plotting something.

If they see me here, who knows what they'll tell everyone?

She skirted the edge of the crowd, although in a town the size of Moss Hollow, it was impossible for her to move in anonymity. Gordon Brett stood a few feet from everyone else, both arms folded across his chest as if he were made of stone. His gaze was pinned on the bakery, eyes glittering. He never turned, never even moved. A shiver slipped down her spine.

From the sidewalk beyond him, someone approached, her presence catching Jillian completely off guard. Surely her best friend wasn't there to support the new bakery or get free coffee and doughnuts, was she?

"Hey girl," Savannah said when she reached Jillian. "Bertie said you'd be here, and I thought you might need a friend beside you."

Of course that's why she came. Savannah Cantrell was loyal to the very center of her soul, and Jillian chastised herself for her momentary lapse in judgment.

"Thank you." She gave Savannah's hand a quick squeeze. "I was just leaving before anyone saw me."

"You don't think anyone has seen you already?"

"I hope not."

"Bless your deluded little heart, Jillian. You're not invisible, not with that red hair."

Jillian sighed and glanced around. Nearly every face was known to her, many of them friends and customers. "I know. I hope no one makes the wrong assumptions about why I'm here. Bertie asked me to come and eye the competition, and that's what I've done."

"And?"

She groaned. "Those dream dollhouses we used to gush over have nothing on this place. You should see—"

The music died and microphone feedback pierced the air.

"May I have your attention?" They looked toward the building to see Mayor Carl Blackwater at the mic. A large man, he was flanked by Megan Farley on one side and two identical willowy redheads on the other. The crowd grew quiet. "It's good to see y'all here this morning. I believe I see some sticky fingers and lips out there." Soft laughter passed through crowd. "The doughnuts and coffee we've been given today have put a shine on our morning. I love seeing the citizens of our town come together. Makes me proud to be part of Moss Hollow, Georgia." He waited until the smattering of applause ceased. "It's an honor for me, as your mayor, to turn the festivities over to a woman who really needs no introduction. She's already made a name for herself in Moss Hollow. Please welcome the executive director of the Moss Hollow Chamber of Commerce, Ms. Megan Farley." He made a slight bow and stepped back.

"Woohoo!" a woman near the front shrieked. "Go, Megan!"

"Only one person I know who could be that animated at a ribbon-cutting, grand-opening ceremony," Savannah said drily.

"Leslie Phipps?"

They moved farther from the crowd, gaining a better view of the podium and those who were nearest to it.

"Exactly," Savannah said. "She's really gaga over Megan, isn't she?"

"She goes gaga over anyone. Always has. I can't help but feel sorry for her."

"Me either. But she can wear you out, for sure, with all that intensity." Savannah made a face and shook herself.

Jillian laughed. "At least Hunter isn't here."

"You didn't think he would be, did you?"

"Not really. But it seems nearly everyone else is."

"In case you haven't noticed," Savannah said with a raised eyebrow, "Hunter isn't 'everyone else.'"

"I've noticed. I'm sorry. That sounded awfully inclusive and snarky, didn't it? Like you, Hunter's been great since the news of Confections & Donuts came out."

Their attention was pulled back to the podium as Megan stepped up to the microphone while applause went up around her. She completely ignored the eager volunteer who now pressed forward, bouncing on her toes and clapping.

"Thank you, Mayor Blackwater. It has been my great privilege to be a part of Moss Hollow these past eight months. As you know, growth can be slow in small towns, especially those towns where some citizens resist change rather than embrace it. But as I've said more than once, the twenty-first century is here, and our community needs to be part of it."

Jillian leaned over and whispered, "She told me that the world is going corporate, and Moss Hollow has to follow."

Savannah curled her upper lip in a sneer. "As *if.*"

The expression of derision, so popular when they were younger, made Jillian giggle loudly enough to cause several people to turn and look at her. She bent her head and studied the ground until she was sure they had focused their attention on Megan once more.

"By welcoming such a dynamic and popular company as Confections & Donuts," the woman said, "Moss Hollow has taken that first important step into progress and economic growth. The first step, I should add, of many."

Her words were greeted with a mixed reaction of polite applause, murmurs of uncertainty, and some restless shifting within the crowd. Neither Megan nor the mayor had mentioned the fire that had destroyed several thousands of dollars' worth of property and materials. As of yet, no one knew much about the origins of the fire, or who, if anyone was responsible. All the public had been told was that it was "suspicious." Jillian had run into the fire chief at the grocery store one afternoon and asked him. His answer had been, "When we know more, we'll let the pubic know." Apparently no one knew anything. Or maybe property owners and the authorities preferred to sweep the catastrophe under the rug.

"Before the ribbon is cut, I'd like to introduce you to Moss Hollow's newest business owners, two lovely women who will be an asset to our town." She beckoned to the twins. "This pair comes to us all the way from Houston, Texas, where they own two Confections & Donuts shops. Each woman holds a business degree, and they have received numerous awards for their efforts. Please give Alyce Sherman and Breanna Sherman a warm Moss Hollow welcome. Oh, and did I mention they are sisters?"

The remark received a laugh as the onlookers applauded. The twin nearest Megan took the huge scissors from her as the other stepped nearer to the microphone.

"Thank you, Ms. Farley. And thank you, citizens of Moss Hollow. I am Alyce Sherman." She paused and offered a toothy smile to everyone. "We cannot begin to express our utter delight at becoming a part of this lovely, picturesque community. Moss Hollow is a charming village, full of wholesome and affable people."

"She sounds about as genuine as paste jewelry," Savannah said near Jillian's ear. The two of them snickered. The more Alyce Sherman spewed uncommon, flowery praise and the longer her sister stood with a brilliant smile pasted on her face, the more tickled Savannah and Jillian became. Jillian grabbed Savannah's hand and rushed her across the street away from the crowd.

"Have you ever heard such ear-curling nonsense in your life?" Her giggle sent Savannah into fresh paroxysms, and they nipped through the nearest doorway, away from curious stares.

"Well now, it's not often we get pretty young ladies in here." Rome Hampstead was standing at the window looking out at the crowd. His snow-white fringe contrasted with his shiny dark pate. His barbershop was devoid of customers, another victim of the happenings across the street. "What brings you two into my shop?"

"I c-can't stop. That voice won't leave my head." Jillian gasped for air between uncontrollable bouts of laughter.

"We're sorry," Savannah choked out. "We don't even know why exactly . . ."

"But we can't help it." Jillian took in a few deep breaths, trying to calm her urge to laugh. A glance at Savannah started it all over again.

Rome stood, arms folded over his sizable middle, watching them. He gave them a brilliant white grin.

"If I was to offer y'all some bubble gum, would you like that?"

They nodded, as eager as a couple of ten-year-olds. He pulled two wrapped pieces of gum from his pocket and handed them over.

"Could I interest either one of y'all in a trim?"

"Just our mustaches," Savannah chirped. The two fell into each other, cackling and snorting.

"S-stop." Jillian waved her hand in front of her face. "D-don't make m-me laugh anymore. I think I feel sick."

Rome went into a backroom and returned with two bottles of cold water. "Here. Try this."

"Thank you," they said. By the time they'd consumed several sips, they had begun to regain some sense of decorum. Jillian's face and stomach muscles ached, and Savannah's face was sunburn-red.

"That gal over there say something funny to get you started?" Rome looked across the street.

Jillian drew in another deep breath and forced her muscles to relax. "Not really. You know how sometimes it's really inconvenient, but you get the urge to laugh and you can't help yourself?"

"And someone is with you, and they do it too?" Savannah unwrapped the big chunk of pink gum and popped it into her mouth.

"I think I know what you mean. Like when you think of something funny during a church service or in the doctor's waiting room."

"Exactly."

"Happened to me once at a funeral service when I was a kid," he said. "I thought my mama was gonna tan my hide for that one."

"I think our giggle-fest came from a lot of tension that has built up lately," Jillian said, "because neither Megan Farley nor Alyce Sherman said anything funny."

"Not in the least. Just foolish."

"Reckon all of you out at Belle Haven are plenty worried about that new bakery," Rome put in.

"You could say that. The servers at the grand opening are pretty insistent that everyone try a doughnut. For a minute, I thought one girl was going to cram one down my throat."

"You mean you didn't take it?" Rome's black eyes twinkled.

"No, sir, I did *not.*"

"You should have."

"Savannah Cantrell, how can you say that?"

"I say that because you need to be familiar with the competition," Savannah explained patiently. "That's why Bertie sent you to the grand opening, wasn't it?"

Jillian winced. "You're right. I didn't even think about it that way. I was just so ticked off by her whole pink-and-white approach, telling me how much better their doughnuts were than what 'you'll find across town.'" Her phone rang. "Excuse me. Hey, Bertie."

"Well? How's it going?"

"I'll be at The Chocolate Shoppe in a few minutes, so I'll fill you in when I get there. I think Savannah is coming with me." She shot her friend a pleading look and received a thumbs-up.

"All right then." Without another word, the phone went dead.

"We'd better scoot, Savannah." Jillian held up her gum. "Thank you, Rome, for the the sanctuary of your shop. And the gum." She unwrapped it and finally put it into her mouth. It was soft, sweet, and comforting, taking her back to the days of her youth.

He gave her a toothy grin. "It's always a bright day when two pretty ladies come a-callin.'"

Savannah followed Jillian's white Prius as they went to the bakery and pulled into the back parking area.

"I dread this," Jillian said as they reached the back door.

"I suppose the best thing is to be honest, but gentle."

"Right." Jillian sucked in a deep breath and opened the door.

The Chocolate Shoppe was completely empty, except for Bertie and Lenora. They were sitting at a table near the coffee station, large cups in front of them. They looked at Jillian and Savannah with all the anticipation of hearing a eulogy.

"How about some coffee?" Jillian asked Savannah who nodded. "You two need a refill?"

Without waiting for their answer, she filled a cup for Savannah and topped up the other two, then poured some for herself. She sat down and started to speak, but when she looked into Bertie's fearful blue eyes, the image of the eager, happy crowd at Confections & Donuts filled her mind, and words failed her.

"So what was it like?" Lenora said quietly. "That new place? I go out of my way so I don't have to drive past it."

"I think Jillian described it best when she compared it to our dolls' dream houses from childhood," Savannah replied.

"Say what?"

"It's pink," Jillian said. "Pink and white, like you decorate a four-year-old girl's room. Ruffled valances and swags at the windows—"

"Lots of windows," Savannah put in.

"The building is white with pink trim. It's kind of overwhelming."

"Sounds kinda pretty," Lenora said, then snapped her mouth shut, obviously appalled by her own words.

"It's pretty enough, if you like that kind of thing," Jillian said, patting her hand.

"Better than camouflage and pea green, I reckon," Bertie muttered.

The bell over the front door rang as two women entered.

"Well, lookee there," Lenora said. "You two been to the new place yet?"

Maudie and Wanda Jean assumed expressions of wide-eyed innocence.

"Why would you ask that?" Maudie said. "You know we love The Chocolate Shoppe."

"So that smear of icing on your chin isn't from one of those free doughnuts they were handing out over there?" Savannah asked. The woman wiped her chin and glowered at her.

"Free doughnuts?" Bertie shook her head. "Can't say I'm surprised."

"You shouldn't be," Wanda Jean said. "You ought to be giving stuff away too."

Bertie blinked at her, and Lenora threw up both hands. "Help this world." She ambled toward the kitchen, shaking her head and muttering about "expectations and foolishness."

"They were handing out samples of fudge and caramels too," Maudie said. "I gotta say, Bertie, you better get on the stick if you don't want to lose your business." She frowned at the coffeepot. "Say, Jillian, there's not enough left in this pot to wet a postage stamp. You want to make some more?"

No, I do not. She did it anyway.

She returned to the table and sat down, reaching for her grandmother's hand. "We'll work this out, Bertie. Try not to worry. And don't listen to—" She made a small motion with her head to indicate the two gossipy women who sat a few tables away.

"That's right." Savannah leaned forward and covered Bertie's other hand. "We'll get through this."

It touched Jillian's heart that Savannah was so close to them she considered herself family. She was always there, rejoicing with them in the best of times and weeping with them during tragedy. She would stick with the Belle Haven women through this situation too.

Lenora came out of the kitchen, balancing plates of pastries. "Here you go." She settled two of the plates on Wanda Jean and Maudie's table. "Free bear claws and doughnut holes, courtesy of your *good friends* at The Chocolate Shoppe."

She carried the other plates to Bertie, Jillian, and Savannah. "Made fresh this morning," she said, and added in a lowered voice, "Trust me. You catch more flies with honey."

Maudie squinted toward the coffeepot. "Is it done yet?"

Jillian wanted to ask Maudie if she hadn't had enough free coffee at Confections & Donuts, but she knew her grandmother would scold her and call her unladylike. Not that being scolded and put in her place bothered Jillian, but she disliked it when she disappointed Bertie, especially when Bertie didn't need anything else to be upset about.

The bakery was completely silent, save the faint hiss of Maudie and Wanda Jean's whispers. Jillian wondered why they were there. To see how Bertie was holding up? To taunt and gloat? But that wasn't a fair assumption. Although the two women were notorious busybodies, they weren't purposefully cruel. Neither of them had ever had malicious intent, only misguided notions. And as members of the Sweetie Pies, Jillian knew they were Bertie's friends.

When the coffee finished brewing, Jillian started to get up, but Wanda Jean stood. "I'll get it, honey. You stay with your grandma."

See? She's not a bad person—sometimes she's just thoughtless.

The woman fetched the pot and refilled everyone's cups before serving herself and Maudie.

"Thank you," Bertie said absently.

"It's the least I can do." She touched Bertie's shoulder with her free hand. "We've been friends for a long time, Bertie—"

"And customers."

"Yes. And customers. Far too long to turn our backs on you for that new shiny place."

Bertie said nothing.

"We had to check them out, Bertie," Maudie added. "If Neiman Marcus came to town, we'd have to check them out too, but we'd still buy most of our clothes from Darcy at Walter's Closet. You know that."

When Bertie remained silent, Jillian said quietly. "We know, Maudie."

"We meant no harm," Maudie insisted.

"Of course not." Wanda Jean set the coffeepot back in place.

Bertie blew out a big breath. "It might be time for me to retire. Maybe Jillian is better suited to handle The Chocolate Shoppe now."

Wanda Jean dropped the two pink packets of sweetener she'd just taken from the coffee station. Lenora sat back as if a cold wind had blown her there.

"Bertie!" Jillian said. Everyone gaped at her grandmother.

Bertie stared at nothing for a long moment, then nodded. "Yep. It just might be that time."

She got up and walked out. A few seconds later, they heard the back door close.

"She doesn't mean that," Jillian said frantically. "I'm not ready to take over the bakery yet."

"Of course she doesn't mean it. She's just upset," Savannah said.

"I don't know." Lenora looked heavenward, as if seeking divine intervention or wisdom. "I've known Bertie a long time, and I've never seen her like this. When she gets down, she picks herself up again right quick. Bertie isn't one to wallow."

"The morning after she collapsed, I saw her hiding a notebook under the covers. I thought maybe she was formulating some kind of strategy to meet this new development, but I guess it was a diary, not a plan."

"Didn't you take a look?"

"No, Lenora, I did not. If Bertie wanted me to know what she was writing, she would have shared it with me."

Lenora sniffed. "I would've looked."

Jillian glanced toward the back of the shop. "I wonder where she is. I better go check on her."

"Ask her about that book she tried to hide from you."

But when Jillian reached the back door, Bertie was gone and so was the bakery's van. Jillian hurried back into the bakery.

"I'm going to go look for her."

"Call her cell phone," Savannah suggested.

"She won't answer if she's in a mood."

"Or if she's driving," Lenora added.

Jillian drove straight across town to Confections & Donuts, fearing Bertie had gone there. If she had, she'd see the crowds of customers.

In her state of mind right now, if she sees all those people, she might actually give up on the bakery. And if she gives up on the bakery . . . She shuddered just thinking of it.

She slowed as she neared the new business, her gaze scouring the landscape for Bertie's vehicle, but she didn't see it. A drive through town produced no results, so she headed to Belle Haven.

Bertie was in the backyard, dressed in a pair of overalls, grubbing in the dirt with Cornelia. Both women were on their knees, but sat up as she approached.

"What are you doing here?" Bertie asked.

"If you want to work in the fern bed over yonder," Cornelia said, "you'll need to change your clothes."

"I'm not here to work, Aunt Cornelia. I've been looking for my grandmother." She pinned a stare on Bertie. "Why did you walk out and tell no one where you were going? We got worried when you didn't come back. I drove all over town trying to find you."

Bertie returned to her task of loosening the soil. "I need to think, Jillian."

"I've been telling you and telling you, there's no better way to think than when your hands are in the dirt." Cornelia lifted her hands, showing dirt-encrusted gloves.

"It would help, *sister dear*, if you'd stop talking while I'm trying to think."

"The way you say 'sister dear' makes me think you'd rather be calling me 'knucklehead.'"

Bertie set her jaw and said nothing else. She refused to look at either of them. Jillian studied both women.

"Aunt Cornelia, I've had an awful craving for some of your raisin-pecan bread pudding. Would you make some for tonight's dessert?"

"Tonight?"

Jillian gave her a bright, expectant smile, hoping Cornelia would take the bait. "It's been quite a while since we've had it."

Cornelia's eyes took on a faraway expression. "Let's see. I don't think I have enough bread, but I probably have everything else."

"I'll get some bread from the bakery. I'm pretty sure there'll be—" She broke off when she realized what had been about to eject from her mouth.

"There'll be plenty," Bertie said without looking up. "Tomorrow it'll be day-old, and a day or two after that, it'll be on its way to turning stale. We don't use that junk to preserve it, like the big bakeries do. Go get what you need. And take her with you." She pointed a small trowel at her sister.

Cornelia frowned at Bertie. "Leave you here all alone?"

Bertie closed her eyes. "Yes, please. I need some quiet."

"But will you be all right?"

"Mercy! I will be fine. Go with Jillian. Teach her how to dry the bread and make the pudding. *Please.*"

Cornelia twisted her mouth, then stood and pulled off her gloves. She brushed the earth from her clothes. "We aren't wanted around here, Jillian. I'll go wash up and then we can go."

"I'm worried about your grandma," Cornelia said as they headed toward the bakery a few minutes later. "I've never seen her this way before."

"Neither have I."

"But this whole mess with Doughboys and Conventions—"

"It's Confections & Donuts, Aunt Cornelia."

Cornelia waved one hand dismissively. "I know, but I'm not going to give them the satisfaction of me calling it that."

"They'll never know what you call it unless you tell them."

Cornelia smiled with a touch of prim superiority. "And I don't care, after them causing my sister all this trouble. Why didn't they open a store in Waycross, or Darien, or Brunswick?"

"Maybe they have."

Cornelia sniffed. "Maybe so. I'll tell you one thing, though. If that place is allowed to stay, our little town is done for."

Supper that evening was a quiet affair, with baked pork chops, cheesy scalloped potatoes, green beans seasoned with bacon and onions, mustard greens, and the bread pudding. Hoping to add a little beauty to the dreary day, Jillian had set the table in the dining room, complete with spring flowers from Cornelia's garden.

Savannah had joined them, and what little conversation was made before dessert was mostly her soothing voice making small talk. Bertie picked at food, rarely looking up.

"I'll go get the bread pudding now." Cornelia pushed back her chair. Full of cinnamon, raisins, and pecans, and topped with a rich buttery sauce, Cornelia's bread pudding was always a favorite at home and community potluck dinners. "Jillian, you made the topping, so you come spoon it on."

When they brought back with four generous, fragrant portions on a silver serving tray, they found Savannah sitting alone at the table.

"She excused herself a minute ago and went to her bedroom."

Uh-oh. It's never a good sign when Bertie turns in before sundown.

"Dear, dear, dear." Cornelia set all four dessert servings in front of Savannah, and stared in the direction of Bertie's room.

"She hardly ate anything." Jillian put the empty tray on the sideboard. "I'll go check on her."

Before she reached the bedroom door, it opened and Bertie came out. She carried a notebook and several pens in her hand. Without a word, she settled in her chair, put the notebook to the side and neatly lined up four ballpoint pens on top of it.

"You going to eat all that, Savannah?" she asked, eyeing the four bowls.

"Huh?" Savannah blinked at the dessert, then smiled. "I just might if it stays where it is now. Here." She passed around the bowls.

"Sit down, you two." Bertie sounded so much like her usual self that Jillian sat quickly, watching her grandmother's face, hoping for more signals she was returning to normal.

"Now, we're going to eat this wonderful bread pudding, then we're going to have a meeting."

The other three exchanged looks.

"What kind of meeting?" Cornelia asked.

"A business meeting. A family meeting. A much-needed meeting." Bertie pinned a look on Savannah. "And you are included in all this, honey. We need you."

"All right."

They ate in silence until Bertie said, "I believe you outdid yourself on this bread pudding, Cornelia."

"Jillian begged for lots of pecans in it. She knew we didn't have any shelled, and so I had to shell them myself while she dillydallied. Not that I'm complaining, mind you."

"You can't have too many pecans, can you, Jillian?" Bertie smiled and winked at her. The task had kept Cornelia busy in the kitchen most of the afternoon, giving Bertie the solitude and quiet she had asked for.

As soon as they finished their desserts, Jillian cleared the table. When she returned to the dining room, Bertie had torn a few pages from her notebook and laid some at everyone's place. She handed each of them a pen, then opened her notebook, straightened her spine, squared her shoulders, and cleared her throat loudly.

"This meeting will come to order." She rapped her knuckles three times against the tabletop.

"For pity's sake," Cornelia said. "We used to play this as kids. I'm in no mood for games tonight."

"Sit down." Bertie frowned at her. "You're out of order."

"I am sitting, and I'm not out of order."

"You were fixing to get up, I could tell. I can read you like a book."

They glared at each other for a bit, then Cornelia blew out a breath. "Okay, okay. But Possum doesn't like the aura in here. Look at him."

Across the room, the cat sat with his tail wrapped around his legs, the tip twitching rhythmically, up and down, up and down, as if it were battery-powered. He regarded them through half-closed lids.

"He looks bored stiff to me," Bertie said. "And fat. You're feeding him way too much bacon."

Cornelia all but hissed at her. "Raymond is not fat. He takes care of himself."

"Maybe Raymond does—or *did*—but *you* are feeding that cat too much. Now, please focus. We're not here to talk about Raymond or Possum, or even bread pudding."

Cornelia fidgeted as if she might speak or even leave. Jillian nudged her gently with her foot under the table and silently signaled her to listen.

"I want to talk to you about the future," Bertie continued.

Cornelia stopped wriggling and turned her full attention on her sister. She rested her fine-boned hands on the table, fingers laced.

"Go on, Bertie," Jillian said quietly.

Bertie took in a deep breath, and as she let it out, she passed around a look that landed on each of them for a few seconds.

"I've been giving this matter of the new bakery a lot of thought, as you probably have guessed."

"We knew something wasn't right, the way you acted," Cornelia said. "You all but threw me out of the house today—"

"Aunt Cornelia, let's listen. Okay?"

"Yes. All right." She leaned back in her chair, but looked ready to leap to her feet at a moment's notice. Jillian covered one of Cornelia's cold, trembling hands and squeezed it tenderly.

"I've given you each a piece of paper and a pen, but don't feel compelled to use them. In fact, hand them back. I don't even know why I gave them to you." Bertie held out her hand, beckoning with her fingers.

"I think I'll just keep mine," Savannah said. "I like to doodle and take notes during meetings."

"So do I." Jillian pulled her paper closer and squeezed Cornelia's hand.

"Me too."

Bertie gave them another sharp look. "Stubborn bunch of women."

"Yes, we are." Savannah smiled beatifically. "All of us."

"Yes. Well." She looked down at the open page of her notebook. "Here's the thing. No matter how you look at it, The Chocolate Shoppe can't begin to put out the volume and variety of treats that Confections & Donuts can, even if we were to open earlier and stay later. Write that down."

Jillian scribbled the words and refrained from saying that working longer hours was the last thing Bertie should be doing.

"I realize I'm no spring chicken," Bertie said, as if she'd read Jillian's thoughts, "and I admit I get tired more quickly than I used to."

"You want us to write that down too?" Cornelia asked. "Is 'spring chicken' one word, or two?"

"Aunt Cornelia." Jillian frowned at her.

Bertie cleared her throat loudly and continued. "I don't find being on my feet an extra several hours a day appealing on any level." She glanced at her notebook again, running her finger down a list she'd written. "Besides, more business hours would mean we'd need to make more food. Write it." She wriggled her index finger at their pages. "There's only so much that our small bakery can do. We'd need more fryers and more ovens. Where would we put them? Upstairs with Lenora? I think not. So let's consider advertising."

"What advertising? Bertie, you don't advertise. Everyone knows The Chocolate—"

"Cornelia, *please*. Let me speak." She glowered at her twin for a moment. "As I was about to say, if we extend hours and make more food, we'd have to advertise, to let people know. Advertising takes money."

"But you'd make it back in sales," Savannah said. "Not that I like the idea of you working yourself to death to compete with Confections & Donuts, but advertising does tend to pay for itself in the long run."

"Thank you, Savannah." Bertie made a little tick on her paper.

"We could cater more parties. Bigger parties. Fancier parties." Cornelia leaned forward. "Parties for debutantes. Balls. We could get a second van and go to bigger cities. We could branch out and do society weddings, themed parties, you name it." Her smile was as soft and wistful as the tone in her voice.

Bertie groaned deep in her throat.

"Aunt Cornelia, that's a lovely dream, but all that would take oodles of time and pocketsful of cash. We need to think of something we can do right away."

Cornelia wilted a little. "Of course. I got carried away."

Bertie looked down at her list, studying it as if it were information she had never seen before. She exhaled slowly and turned the page, then looked up. "I believe it's best we move to Plan B."

"What is Plan B?" Savannah asked.

"I believe the answer to this dilemma, for us and The Chocolate Shoppe, is quite simple." She swallowed hard. "That is, before that new place swallows us whole and causes us all kinds of problems, I—uh, I believe . . ." She cleared her throat, then sat up straight. "I believe the best thing for me to do is to hang up my apron. It's time. In fact, it might be past time."

Jillian had expected this. If Bertie had opened up and talked with her earlier, she might have been able to derail the notion before it fully bloomed in her grandmother's head. Once Bertie got hold of an idea, it was hard for her to let go. Jillian hoped she could redirect Bertie's despair and resignation into enthusiasm for something else.

"Let's not be hasty," she said.

"No, please don't." Savannah reached out and caught Bertie's forearm. "Surely there is something we can do. Let's go back to your first ideas and rethink how to make them work."

Bertie continued as if she hadn't heard. "Most women my age aren't getting up before daylight and working eight, ten, twelve hours a day. No sir. They're sleeping as late as they want, then getting up and watching *The Price Is Right* or *Dr. Phil* in their bathrobes while eating breakfast and sipping coffee. Besides, Cornelia can use some help around here. Belle Haven's upkeep is too much for one old woman."

"What? Who are you calling old?" Cornelia said, looking outraged. "Don't I keep this place clean? Don't I cook good meals? And I'm making progress with those gardens out there, right? Do you think all I do is watch TV in my bathrobe?"

"I did not say that. You *know* I did not say that."

"You might not have said it, but it's what I heard." Cornelia sniffed indignantly and turned away, arms folded.

"For Pete's sake!" Savannah said, surprising everyone. Usually, Savannah was always a quiet, nearly placid presence in the house. They all gaped at her.

"I don't believe I've ever heard you raise your voice before," Cornelia said.

"Neither have I." Bertie frowned. "Are you upset?"

"Yes, I'm upset. You two are sniping at each other like you're eight instead of eighty. Instead of acting like children, you need to be directing your energy toward saving your business. Cornelia, you should listen more than talk, and Bertie, you should open up instead of keeping everything to yourself. Let's agree that Confections & Donuts is the problem, and it's not going away. We need to fight. Bertie, if you retire, The Chocolate Shoppe has no chance at all. So let's focus on what we can do to help it survive. All right?"

The twins looked at her wide-eyed and nodded.

"Hear, hear!" Jillian slapped the flat of her hand against the tabletop and grinned at her friend. If she were to score how much she treasured Savannah's wisdom and friendship on a scale from one to ten, it would be at least fifteen.

Bertie shifted, sniffled, and blinked a couple of times. "Have either of you got any ideas for if I choose not to retire?"

"Jillian could take over now instead of later." Cornelia looked as if she'd just announced a free and legal alternative to gasoline. "Why didn't we think of that before?"

"We have thought of that before, but that doesn't solve the problem, Aunt Cornelia. The bakery will still be the same size and in the same place, and Confections & Donuts will still be the big boy across town."

Cornelia sat back, deflated.

"Bertie, you mentioned more ovens and fryers," Jillian said. "What about expanding the kitchen?"

"I don't see how, unless we cut back on seating space."

"Build onto the back. That space isn't used for anything but our parking and the dumpster."

"I think that's a brilliant idea." Savannah gave Jillian a big smile. "Put in a new kitchen back there and expand the current seating area into the existing kitchen."

Bertie chewed on her lower lip. "But that will be costly. You seem to forget that Belle Haven still needs several things repaired or replaced, and the taxes aren't getting any cheaper."

Cornelia's face pinched. "Oh, dear. Will we have to choose between our home and The Chocolate Shoppe?"

"Aunt Cornelia, I did not say we should do this, especially not right away. But it's something to think about."

"It won't cost anything to talk to a contractor and get an estimate," Savannah said.

"You're right." Bertie pointed her finger at the paper in front of Jillian. "Write it down so you won't forget."

"I just hope no one burns up *our* building supplies." Everyone looked at Cornelia.

"Why on earth would someone do that?" Bertie asked.

"How should I know? But it happened across town. I just hope it doesn't happen to us." Cornelia scooted back her chair and got up, her expression preoccupied. "Possum and I need to have a little confab. Something doesn't feel right."

Bertie rolled her eyes and waved Cornelia away while Jillian and Savannah averted their gazes and kept their faces expressionless.

"I will never understand my sister," she said with a sigh when Cornelia was out of earshot.

"But we love her anyway."

"Of course we do, Jillian. It's just that her foolishness exasperates me to no end at times, and right now, I've had just about as much exasperation as I can stand."

"I know, Bertie."

"We're here to help you," Savannah said. "Both of you."

"All of us," Jillian added.

"That includes Possum and Raymond, I suppose," Bertie said, her eyes twinkling.

"It does."

They laughed together, but then Bertie lost her humor and her face folded into weariness and worry.

"I guess this meeting is over. At least for now." She began gathering the pens and paper, and glanced at Savannah. "Thanks for being here, honey. We consider you a part of the family, you know."

"I know, and I love it. Thanks for dinner. It was really good." She stood. "I hate to bail out, but I have an early day tomorrow, and I am dead tired. I should get going unless you have further need of me."

"No, no. You go on home, if you want to. I'm about to turn in early myself."

Dusk had deepened nearly to dark when Jillian walked her friend out to the car. A breeze caught and stirred the scent of the waxy, thick-petaled magnolia blossoms. She breathed in the fragrance.

"I am so glad you were here this evening, Savannah. I don't know if I could have handled all of this by myself."

"Sure you could have, but I'm glad I was here. I think it helped to have us both encouraging her not to retire, especially since it's clear she really doesn't want to. Considering her first two suggestions—advertising and more equipment—I think Bertie wants to keep working. I think she wanted us to talk her out of retirement."

Jillian moved a pebble in the driveway with the toe of her shoe and didn't look up when she said, "That's true. But all things considered, do you think Bertie *ought* to retire?"

"You mean because she's eighty?"

"She's robust and healthy, but she's not getting any younger. I'm also thinking of the amount of stress she could let escape if she did. Pressure is bad for a person, no matter their age."

Savannah arched an eyebrow. "Do you really think Bertie

would be less stressed knowing you were trying to handle all the pressures of running a small bakery against a large one by yourself and she could do nothing to help?"

"I guess not. But still, think about it. Even if we make the changes, chances are good the bakery will still suffer, if not fail, because of Confections & Donuts."

She looked up to discover Savannah studying her face. "With an attitude like that, The Chocolate Shoppe is beaten before it starts. I didn't realize you thought that way, Jillian."

Her tone was gentle, but it still felt like a reproach.

"I didn't. I mean, I don't. I mean, I'm not sure what to think, other than I feel as if I'm teetering on the edge of a cliff that might give way at any moment."

"I understand, and I wish I knew what to tell you other than to try not to worry. Things are going to change, but that change doesn't have to be bad. In fact, change is usually good."

"I suppose it's the way we look at it, meet it, and deal with it that helps us grow from it. Certainly I've been through plenty of changes in my life, and without those changes, I wouldn't be here in Moss Hollow."

"And that would be a shame." Savannah smiled her sweet smile, then looked out over the grounds. Suddenly she stiffened, her gaze pinned to something on the far side of the front lawn.

"What's wrong?"

"I saw someone over there."

Jillian turned and scoured the darkening landscape. "I don't see any—"

"It's Gordon." Savannah clutched her arm and lowered her voice to a whisper. "He just stepped out of sight on the other side of that magnolia tree."

Jillian relaxed. "You know he doesn't drive. He's probably walking home from somewhere."

"He wasn't walking when I spotted him. He was standing over there, staring at Belle Haven. Look, there he is now."

Jillian watched as a shadowy figure flitted across her line of vision and disappeared. She squinted hard into the darkness.

"Are you sure it was Gordon?"

"Yes, I recognized his hat. No one but him would wear a white straw hat at night."

"Where'd he go?"

"I don't know." Savannah leaned forward, trying to see.

"Let's find out what he's up to. Come on." Jillian grabbed Savannah's hand and pulled her along.

Together, they moved away from the lights of Belle Haven and slipped into the shadows of the night.

"Why is he skulking out here in the dark?" Jillian said.

"He's probably upset that we talked to the sheriff about him."

Jillian stopped and turned to her. "You did?"

"Yes. Didn't you?"

"Only after the sheriff came here, asking questions."

"Gordon came here that night I joined y'all for dinner with those petitions of his, and then a few nights later there was that fire. You know as well as I do that if you know or suspect something about a crime you're supposed to tell the authorities. So I went to Coy Henderson and told him about Gordon's visit. Didn't he tell you?"

"No, and neither did you until this minute."

"I thought you would have guessed and done the same."

"He came out and asked us some questions about Gordon, but he didn't even mention you. What do you expect, though? Our sheriff uses words like they cost a hundred dollars apiece. But we're wasting time. Come on."

By the time the pair reached the road that passed in front of Belle Haven, they had spotted nobody and saw no other movement.

"Where did he go?" Jillian whispered.

"Beats me. But he was there. You saw him, didn't you?"

"I saw someone. I thought it was a person, but maybe it was just tree limbs waving in the breeze or something."

"No, there was enough light where he was that I saw him." Savannah said flatly. "It was Gordon Brett."

"Hey, Gordon, you out here?" Jillian called.

Savannah gaped at her. "What are you doing?" she hissed.

"I'm trying to find out why our neighbor is sneaking around out here at night," Jillian replied in a normal voice. "He's not done that before."

"That you know of. What are we going to do if we find him?"

"Ask him what he's up to, of course."

"What if we find him, and he's angry because we talked with the sheriff and he turns violent?"

"Are you kidding? It's *Gordon*. I don't think he even eats meat. Come on." She moved forward, Savannah lagging behind a couple of steps.

"We don't have anything to defend ourselves with, Jillian."

She was glad it was dark so Savannah could not see her roll her eyes. "If he turns mean, then I'll holler and jump on his back, and you kick him."

Savannah groaned. "You have a lot of Aunt Cornelia in you after all."

Jillian stopped so suddenly Savannah ran into her. "Take that back."

"I won't. Cornelia is imaginative and tenacious, and so are you. That's all I'm saying."

"Huh. I think you might be implying that I'm a little bit of a featherbrain sometimes."

Savannah huffed. "I'm not saying another word. Except I think this is a foolish expedition."

"Then feel free to go back to your car and go home. I'm not afraid of Gordon."

"So you're going to keep looking for him, in the dark, without a flashlight, and without a weapon?"

"Yep." She started to move on.

"You beat all, Jillian Green." She sighed again, this time with resignation. "I'm not letting you get yourself murdered all by yourself. Lead on. I do hope you realize, though, that I'm sacrificing my Tory Burch shoes for this silliness."

"I'm sorry, but it's a little too late to worry about that now. I hope you don't step in something awful."

"Gee, thanks."

The two crept forward, stalled somewhat by shrubs, flower beds, and unexpected dark shapes that shifted in the rapidly fading light. They paused often to peer around, and Jillian called for Gordon a few times, always to be met with silence.

"If we walk along the road, we won't be so apt to step on a copperhead," Savannah said at one point.

"Snakes. Yikes, I didn't think about them." Jillian made a sharp left and headed toward the country road that would lead them to Gordon Brett's house. They walked along the shoulder, rarely speaking. The night was quiet and peaceful, and no cars had passed them by the time they arrived at Gordon's driveway. His home was completely dark.

"We aren't going there, are we?" Savannah asked.

"Why not? If he was sneaking around Belle Haven, there must have been a reason, and I want to know what it was."

Pretending to be far grittier and braver than she felt, Jillian strode toward the house. Savannah hurried to catch up.

"What are we going to do when we get there?"

"Talk to him, of course. What have I been saying?"

"Just like Cornelia," Savannah muttered. Jillian ignored her.

The moonlight was enough to light the pathway through various vegetable and herb patches to his front door. Jillian turned the tarnished brass key that rang the old-fashioned doorbell.

"It's at this point in slasher movies that crazed killers stand behind their victims, axes raised."

"For Pete's sake, Savannah. You've never been this lily-livered before. Gordon is not a crazed killer, with or without an axe."

Still, she cast a quick glance behind them. She felt silly when she saw nothing. She rang the bell again. When Gordon failed to answer after the third ring and several knocks, she didn't know whether to be relieved or irritated.

"He's not home," she said, turning away.

"That, or he knows we're here and he's refusing to come to the door."

Jillian passed her gaze over the darkened gardens and beyond, saw nothing change. "Maybe. I'll come over tomorrow."

"I wish you'd decided to do that before we made this little excursion. I'm tired and need to get up early in the morning, remember?"

Maybe it was the way the moonlight hit her face and created smudged shading beneath her eyes, but she did look weary. Savannah had always been full of vigor and nerve. This new side of her, cautious and even timid, caught Jillian by surprise. Guilt stabbed her conscience, and she wanted to set Savannah's mind at ease, if nothing else. She tucked her hand into the crook of her friend's elbow.

"I'm sorry. Sometimes I get a notion in my head and become single-minded."

"I know."

Jillian thought about that for a moment. "Are you about to say that I'm like Aunt Cornelia again?"

"I don't need to say it. You just did."

They walked toward the road. Jillian stumbled, and Savannah caught her before she fell.

And that's what good friends do. She smiled in the dark.

The exhausted Savannah got in her car and headed home as soon as they reached the mansion, but Jillian was still keyed up. Just as she went inside and locked the front door, an unwelcome thought slithered into her mind. What if that person they'd seen outside, whether it was Gordon or not, had slipped into the mansion while they were off chasing after him? That's why they hadn't seen anyone outside, even after their eyes had adjusted to the night. Not only had Savannah's dire "what-ifs" wormed their way into her brain, they had brought a coldness unlike any she'd ever experienced. It formed in her middle and spread until she was breathless and frozen in place.

What if someone has hurt Bertie or Aunt Cornelia?

She swallowed hard, gripped by terrifying images. She willed herself to breathe.

"Bertie?" Her voice had as much substance as a fistful of mist. She licked her dry lips and tried again. "Bertie? Aunt Cornelia?" When neither answered, she ran to Bertie's bedroom door and flung it open without bothering to knock.

Bertie sat straight up in bed with a shriek.

"Bertie, are you all right?" Jillian fumbled for the light switch, then flipped it on.

Her grandmother blinked and gasped, clutching the sheets to her chest. "Jillian! What on earth? Whatever has gotten into you?"

"Are you all right?" Jillian asked again, shooting a wild gaze around the room. She looked under the bed, and peeked in the closet and in the bathroom.

"Of course I'm all right. Other than being terrified out of my sleep. What are you looking for?"

"Where's Aunt Cornelia?"

"I expect she's upstairs in her room, fast asleep. Like I was a moment ago." She threw back the covers and scooted to the edge of the bed, feeling for her slippers with her feet. "What's going on?"

Without replying, Jillian sprinted out of the room and upstairs. She rapped on Cornelia's door but did not wait for an answer. Instead, she opened it wide, letting the hall light spill across the bed. Her aunt snored quietly beneath a lacy white counterpane, Possum curled on the pillow next to her head. He opened one eye and glared at Jillian.

"What are you doing?" Bertie whispered right behind her. "Let her sleep."

Jillian stepped inside and gave Cornelia a hard stare, just to reassure herself the woman was all right, then nodded. She backed out of the room and silently closed the door.

"Don't make me ask you again, Jillian. What is going on?"

Jillian took her arm and led her away from Cornelia's door. "I'll tell you downstairs. I need a cup of tea."

"After this, so do I."

Bertie put the kettle on while Jillian got out the cups and tea bags.

"What would you like, Bertie? Chamomile? Cinnamon Comfort? Nighty-Nite?"

"Regular orange pekoe, decaf."

Bertie showed her age as she moved to the breakfast table and lowered herself by degrees into a chair. It was a rare occasion she moved so slowly or with such obvious stiffness.

"Would you like some toast, Bertie?"

"No, thank you. What I'd like is for you to sit down, right there," she pointed to a chair across from her, "and tell me why you're tearing around here like a mad dog is after you."

Jillian sat on the edge of her seat and tapped one foot. Bertie, who disapproved of fidgeting, frowned at her. She scooted back and tried to relax.

"When Savannah and I were outside, we saw someone in the front yard."

"Who?"

"I'm not sure. Savannah thought it was Gordon Brett because she saw his hat. All I saw was the figure of someone. Just for a few seconds, then he was gone."

"Gone where?"

Jillian shrugged. "I don't know. We looked around for him and saw no one."

Bertie glanced at the kitchen clock. "I've been in bed for over an hour. You couldn't possibly have been out in the front yard all that time. Were you?"

"No, we went looking for him."

"What do you mean you went looking for him?"

"I mean we tried to find him. We figured he slipped into the trees to hide from us, so we went after him."

"Jillian!"

"Bertie, if it was Gordon Brett, I wasn't going to let him lurk around Belle Haven without knowing why, especially as he was being sneaky. When someone is being sneaky, it's almost never good. But we didn't find him in the woods, so we went to his house."

"You went to his house." Bertie echoed the words dully.

"Yes."

"And Savannah went along?"

"Yes, ma'am."

"Mercy, child." Bertie rubbed one temple and shook her head. "Give me one more thing to worry about, why don't you?"

"I'm fine. Savannah is fine. She went home. There's nothing to worry about."

Nothing except someone spying on Belle Haven in the middle of the night.

The teakettle whistled, startling them both. Jillian got up and took it off the flame to pour the boiling water over their tea bags.

"Mercy," Bertie said again. "I'm glad you're home, safe and sound. Do you realize what could have happened?"

"I know. Everything from being clubbed to death with a tree branch to dying of snakebite."

"Or worse."

"It's all right. We followed the road for part of the way, and nothing happened."

"We can thank the good Lord for that. 'Mad dogs and Englishmen'—and foolish Southern girls, apparently."

"Bertie, I'm not a girl. I'm staring down the barrel of a fortieth birthday, for goodness' sake."

Bertie blew on her tea. "One would never know."

Jillian narrowed her eyes. *Was that a compliment or not?* She decided not to ask.

"What did he say? Gordon." Bertie took a careful sip.

"He didn't say anything. He never came to the door."

"Did you knock?"

"What kind of question is that? Of course I knocked. I rang the bell. I called his name."

"I hope you didn't go snooping around his house, looking in windows and under rocks."

"Now why would I do that?"

Bertie sat her cup down with a clink and folded her arms. "I don't understand how your mind works. You chase what you think is our neighbor all over Nathan County in the dark, treading on snakes and who-knows-what, then traipse down the highway where you could have been run over by a truck or something. After all that, I would have expected you to dig around in his tomato plants or crawl in through the kitchen window to prowl around in his house."

Jillian tried to protest, but could think of nothing to say.

Bertie stood up, waving one hand dismissively. "I'm going back to bed. I'll probably dream about you getting strangled. Tomorrow I'm calling Miss Savannah Cantrell and giving her a piece of my mind. I'd've thought she at least had sense enough not to go chasing shadows in the middle of the night." She kept muttering as she left the kitchen, carrying her nearly full cup of tea.

Jillian sat where she was. A number of emotions and ideas tore through her brain, but the one that returned like a bad toothache was the worry that the prowler had not been Gordon Brett. What if that unknown person was out there, right now, watching Belle Haven, getting ready to pounce?

As usual, Bertie left for the bakery before sunrise the next morning. Jillian slipped out unnoticed while Cornelia tidied the kitchen. The air felt fresh and cool. A soft rosiness spread across the sparkling dew-damp lawn. It was a perfect spring morning. If she hadn't been so intent on her purpose, Jillian would have taken some extra time to enjoy the delights of a new day.

She stood on the bottom step of the front porch and gazed across the wide lawn in front of Belle Haven. Cornelia had done a good job with her plans for landscaping, and the man she'd hired kept it trimmed and tidy. It was a labor of love, and Jillian sometimes wondered what her great-aunt would do when the work was done. She shook herself. She needed to look for signs.

But what kind of signs? she asked herself as she strolled across the lawn. *Anything that might prove someone was out here last night.* She tried to figure out where she had seen someone move.

Funny how different everything looks in the dark.

She examined the grass, wondering if she could find shoe prints, but all she saw was even, tender growth. Around the magnolia tree, with its large, fragrant white blooms, she found a single blossom on the ground. Maybe it had fallen off or been knocked off. Or even plucked. She picked it up and buried her nose in the creamy petals, inhaling their sweetness. Her search took her into the woods along the invisible path she thought they had trekked last night, but her search yielded nothing out of the ordinary.

In spite of Savannah's worries and her grandmother's warning, she was not afraid of Gordon Brett. Whether or not he had been skulking outside Belle Haven, Jillian refused to believe he harbored any intent to cause them harm. The only way to assuage that lingering, niggling, annoying doubt in the back of her mind was to confront him, and she fully intended to do so right then, in full light of day.

Her cell phone rang. She glanced at the screen, then answered.

"Everything okay, Bertie?"

"Where are you?"

She glanced around at the trees with birds singing and a couple of squirrels scampering through the branches.

"I'm right here."

"What kind of answer is that? I just now called the house, and Cornelia said your car was still there, but she couldn't find you. When are you coming in to work?"

One thing about the stress of the last few weeks, it had turned her loving grandmother into a fussing, cranky old woman. Bertie Harper might be opinionated and outspoken, but usually she was refined and polite.

"I'll be there soon."

"Well, make it snappy. Grant Bower is coming by directly to talk to us, and it would be nice if you were here."

"Grant Bower, the contractor? I understand he's one of the best in Moss Hollow."

"Yes, he is. He's a busy man, and I don't want to keep him waiting while you dillydally. Get a move on."

There goes my plan to talk to Gordon. She turned and headed toward the house.

"Shall I bring Aunt Cornelia?"

"Not for this initial consultation. She's liable to distract him by asking a lot of unnecessary questions. I'll fill her in when I get home."

"All right. I'll be there in a few minutes."

"Mercy on us, girl," Bertie said when Jillian walked into the bakery. "Did you forget to comb your hair this morning?"

Jillian's hands flew to her hair. She remembered running a brush through it after she got dressed, but Jillian's hair had always had a mind of its own. An early morning walk in Georgia's humid air had encouraged those locks to rebel.

"Bad hair day," she muttered, combing it with her fingers.

"Go fix it before Grant gets here. Goodness knows we don't want to look like street urchins when we talk to him."

"Street urchins? Bertie, you and I would never pass for urchins—"

"Go!"

In the mirror of the bakery's small bathroom, Jillian did her best to tame her hair. Plundering her purse, she found and applied lipstick. She studied her reflection, winced, and went back to the front.

Bertie eyed her critically. "You'll do."

Sunlight flared off a car windshield and splashed along the wall behind them. Bertie glanced toward the parking lot and stiffened. "There he is. You go get the biggest, warmest, cinnamon-pecan sticky buns to come out of the new batch Lenora is taking from the oven. Put it on china, with a real fork not a plastic one." She started to turn away, paused, and added, "And be nice."

Jillian blinked. "I hardly think I'm obnoxious, Bertie, even on my worst days."

"Just be charming. That's all I'm asking." Bertie was as twitchy and nervous as Jillian had ever seen her. Meeting with a contractor shouldn't make anyone so edgy, but Bertie hadn't been herself lately. Jillian gave her a reassuring smile.

"Yes, ma'am. I'll do my best."

In the kitchen, Lenora turned out a large pan of gooey rolls onto a tray covered with parchment paper. The butter, brown sugar, and chopped pecans that had lined the bottom of the pan was now a thick, dark glaze over the fresh cinnamon rolls. They were Bertie's special rolls and had always been Jillian's favorite. Bertie said she didn't make them often because, if she did, they'd soon lose their novelty and become expected. She liked to have some of her offerings to be exceptional. Whenever word got around that she was making cinnamon-pecan gooey rolls, they were always gone well before noon.

"With business being so slow," Jillian said, "Bertie ought to make these every day. No one is going to get tired of them, no matter what she thinks."

Lenora looked at her without lifting her head from the task of spreading the glaze evenly. The result was a hard scowl that came out from beneath her eyebrows.

"Ain't nobody out there to buy anything, not even one of these, in case you didn't notice." She used a spatula to scrape the last bit of drizzle from the pan onto the rolls.

"I saw Stewie Franks in his corner."

Lenora grunted and plunged the empty pan into a steel sink half full of hot soapy water. "That man has one cake doughnut, a cup of coffee, and three free refills every morning while he reads the Atlanta paper. We can't keep The Chocolate Shoppe running on sales like that."

"No, of course not." Jillian got out a white china plate from a stack and carefully chose a roll.

"And there's your grandma all set to expand this place, like she thinks more room will bring in more business. That's the most foolish notion I ever heard in my life."

"Maybe not."

"Maybe not? Girl, if she builds onto this shop, it will take every cent she has and then some. Y'all could lose Belle Haven. Did you think of that?"

Jillian had thought of that. In fact, the mere idea made her sick to her stomach. But if she gave in to fear, her focus would lock on obstacles and she'd fail to see solutions. Fear and failure were bed partners she refused to join.

She got a fork, several napkins, and a china mug. "At this point, she's only talking about it. And meeting with Grant Bower this morning will help her sort it out a bit in her mind."

"Mmhmm." Lenora's expression was as skeptical as her murmur. She folded her arms over her chest.

"I won't let her do anything foolish," Jillian said.

"I don't reckon she needs your permission to be foolish."

"Oh, Lenora."

"You have Grant's roll?" Bertie asked from behind her.

"Yes, Bertie. I have it right here on a real plate, with a real fork. I'll even serve coffee in a real mug."

"Then come along. You are the biggest piddler in the world today." She led the way to a table near the window.

Grant Bower, a solid-built man with dark hair and eyes, stood as they approached. He had gone to school in Moss Hollow and graduated five years before Jillian. He'd been a star athlete, and surprised everyone when he chose to go into business rather than sports. Good-hearted and soft-spoken, he was also a sharp businessman with a reputation for making tough deals.

His eyes lit up when Jillian placed the glistening sticky bun before him, and filled the white mug with fresh, steaming coffee.

"Thank you so much. My favorite."

"Everyone's favorite," she said with a smile.

Maudie and Wanda Jean came into the bakery, chattering

happily. They looked around the nearly empty room, spotted the threesome at the table, and approached.

"Why, Grant Bower!" Maudie said. "I haven't seen you since Hector was a pup."

He stood, smiled, shook their hands, and asked after their general well-being.

"What're you doing here in the middle of the morning? Can we join your party?" Without waiting for consent or invitation, Wanda Jean started to get a chair from another table.

"Actually, this is a business meeting," Jillian said.

"Business?" As if neither one of them had ever heard the word before.

"Yes, ma'am. If you don't mind, we'll get on with it now. Grant's a busy man." Jillian cringed a little at how she sounded, prim and snippy. Not what she intended at all. She got up and poured coffee for them. "What can I get you ladies to go with the coffee?"

"Nothing right now." Maudie sniffed. "Enjoy your business meeting."

They settled at the next table and put their heads together. Jillian didn't want to imagine what they were talking about.

Bertie told Grant what she had in mind, from expanding the dining area to building on to the back of the bakery. Speaking with confidence and authority, she hid her anxieties well. In fact, had Jillian been an outside observer, she'd never have known insecurities and fears plagued her grandmother.

Once Bertie had begun to share her ideas with Grant, Maudie and Wanda Jean both sat erect and silent, eavesdropping to beat the band. If Bertie noticed their attentiveness, she didn't let it show. On the other hand, their interest bothered Jillian. The last thing her grandmother needed was to be inundated with questions and predictions from the two women.

As he ate, Grant listened attentively to Bertie's thoughts for expansion. He nodded from time to time, sipping coffee once the roll was consumed. His questions were concise and easy to understand.

He made notes, then said, "I'd like to have a look at the kitchen, the storage area, and the back of the building."

"Follow me."

Bertie led Grant toward the back of the bakery.

Maudie and Wanda Jean moved as if they were going to follow. Jillian knew it was impossible to keep the Snoop Sisters in the dark for long, but maybe she could appeal to their better natures.

"Ladies, we have Bertie's best rolls today. How about it? One for each of you, on the house?"

Neither Maudie nor Wanda Jean possessed the svelte figures of their youth. They didn't pretend to diet and always greeted sweets and snacks with delight.

"That would be wonderful." Maudie beamed.

"Yes indeed." Wanda Jean all but rubbed her hands together.

When Jillian returned with the rolls, she sat down with the two friends and leaned in close. "Just between us, if Bertie seems distant and distracted, it's because she has a lot on her mind."

"It's that awful place across town, isn't it?" Wanda Jean cut into her warm pastry.

"I'm afraid so."

"Is she making herself sick, honey?" Maudie's eyes were filled with genuine concern.

"She's worried, yes. And why shouldn't she be? Business has slowed to a crawl since Confections & Donuts opened." They looked around the nearly empty bakery. "Talking about that place, or our lack of customers, distresses her even more. So if you could refrain from mentioning it, that would take a load off my mind."

"Of course, hon."

"Our lips are sealed."

Their lips were never truly sealed, but Jillian appreciated the promise. "Thank you."

"Jillian." Lenora beckoned to her from behind the counter.

"Excuse me, ladies. Enjoy your rolls."

Lenora pulled Jillian into the kitchen. "You need to stay right with your grandma so no one hoodwinks or bothers her."

"I will, but Grant Bowers is not the sort to hoodwink her."

"I've got to where I don't trust anyone these days. Better safe than sorry." She slid a glance toward the front, where Maudie and Wanda Jean still enjoyed their rolls. "And let's not let those two get her in an uproar."

"I've talked to them. They promise not to upset her."

"Good. Now get on out there and give that old lady some support."

Jillian stepped out the back door just in time to hear Grant say, "I believe what you want is doable, Miss Bertie. I'll need to do some checking into the structure of the building, find out where utilities come in, that sort of thing. And if you decide to move forward with this we'll have to get permission from the city for the expansion, especially since we'll need to dig up the back parking lot."

Bertie planted her hands on either side of her waist. "If they gave permission for that monstrosity to be built over there on Catalpa, they surely can't turn down a new kitchen on my property."

"Yes, ma'am. I'll be back, probably after you close this evening so I don't disturb your customers, and do my checking then. I'll work up an estimate for you and have that for you soon. Will that suit you?"

"Thank you, Grant." They shook hands, Bertie offering her usual warm smile. "I appreciate you taking the time out of your busy schedule to come over today, especially as it was a bit spur of the moment."

"Miss Bertie, you are one of my favorite people in Moss Hollow. It's never a bother to spend a few minutes with you." He turned to Jillian and shook her hand. "I'll see you ladies later." He strode around the side of the building and was gone.

A long silence followed as they stood gazing at the back of The Chocolate Shoppe.

"Not very pretty from this side, is it?" Bertie asked.

"The backs of most businesses aren't pretty."

"I used to want to build a little patio out here." She indicated an area near them. "Have an umbrella table and few chairs, a nice place to take a break, or have lunch." She paused, her eyes reflecting a memory. "I had a plumbing problem back here once, about fifteen or twenty years ago, give or take. You were in college. What a mess. I hired a couple of fellas to fix it for me, and they did a fine job. Haven't had a problem since." She smiled wistfully at Jillian. "I wished I'd had them build that kitchen back then."

"You didn't know you'd need it."

"True, true." She sighed. "I might not even need it now."

Jillian put one arm around her shoulders. "Let's not think that way."

She refused to admit, even to herself, that her grandmother's fears might not be misplaced.

I will not let this bakery go easily. Not without a fight.

"I wonder what happened to those fellas. They were good, hard workers, but they left town and never came back." They walked toward the back door. "Y'know, I reckon I must be getting old. I can't even remember their names."

Rather than go straight home that evening, Jillian drove to Gordon Brett's house. She expected him to be outside working in his gardens, but he wasn't there.

"Gordon?" she called when she got out of the car. "You home?"

Repeated knocking on his door with no answer raised her concern. She peeked in the windows and saw clean, sparsely furnished rooms, but didn't see him. Maybe he had had an accident on his way from Belle Haven last night and was lying injured somewhere. She set out, cutting across the meadows and woods that separated their two houses, her eyes sharpened for any sign of him on the ground. She called out for him frequently, but after seeking along every possible route he would have taken on foot, she still found no sign of him.

Although he was generally liked in the community, he had few real friends, and no family that she knew of. It was possible the petition he was passing around had garnered him some enemies.

Maybe he hadn't been spying on Belle Haven last night. Maybe he'd been trying to hide from someone.

She hurried back to the car and drove to the sheriff's office.

11

When Jillian walked into The Chocolate Shoppe on Friday morning, Bertie greeted her by waving a newspaper like the final flag at NASCAR.

"Well, this is a fine howdy-do. How do you explain it?"

"Explain what?" Jillian stashed her purse under the counter and grabbed an apron. "Is there something about Gordon? I reported him missing at the sheriff's office, but it's been—"

Bertie shoved that week's edition of the *Moss Hollow Chronicle* into her hands. "No. Nothing about him. Look."

Lenora stood behind Bertie and rubbed a place between her shoulders. Her face was a mask of worry.

Jillian smoothed the pages and read aloud a headline on the front page. "'Moss Hollow Business to Expand in Desperate Attempt to Compete.'"

"Oh, *please*," Bertie said, throwing up both hands.

"Don't read it out loud, sugar. Your grandma is upset enough without hearing the story out loud."

Silently Jillian read the article. It said The Chocolate Shoppe appeared to be on the verge of failure. The piece hinted that Bertie was infirm, possibly senile, and blatantly stated the bakery was struggling with record-low sales since Confections & Donuts had established a modern new business with "superior baked goods." In fact, the last half of the article was more like an advertisement for Confections & Donuts than a news story.

By the time she'd finished reading, Jillian's face and chest were ready to explode, and her breath came in short bursts. When was the last time she had been this furious?

"Who wrote this piece of garbage?" she demanded.

Bertie shook her head, and Lenora said, "We don't know, but I reckon it was Rod Douglas. Don't he usually write most of the pieces in that paper?"

"Did he talk to you about this, Bertie?"

"He did not."

"Wanda Jean and Maudie, the Mouths of the South, were the only ones in the shop when Grant Bower was here," Lenora said.

"No. Stewie was at his usual table over in the corner. Remember?" Bertie looked toward the empty corner.

Lenora snapped her fingers. "That's right. He was." She and Jillian followed Bertie's gaze. "Where do you reckon he is now?"

"If he went running to Rod with my personal business, then he's probably too chicken to show his face."

"That's true." Jillian glared at the corner before reconsidering. "But Stewie is hard of hearing. You really think he could have even heard you? Besides, he's hardly the type to spread rumors."

"She's right, you know." Lenora met Bertie's eyes. "Why, the man takes his hearing aid out so he can read the paper in peace."

"But then where did this come from?" Bertie sank into the nearest chair. "I just don't understand."

Two men entered the bakery and began perusing the goods. The rest of the place was empty of customers. As Lenora waited on the new arrivals, Jillian grabbed her purse from beneath the counter.

"What are you doing, girl? You just got here."

"I'm going to go see Rod Douglas. I'm going to find out who gave him this information, and then I'm going to chew him out for blathering personal information."

"You make him print a retraction." Bertie pointed at the newspaper.

"Don't worry, I'll handle it. See you later."

The last week had stirred up her anger more times than she cared to count.

Not good for my blood pressure, my heart, my stomach, or my face. She blew out a long, slow breath and forced herself to relax. *Not good for public relations either.*

Jillian was still fuming by the time she reached the brick building that housed the *Moss Hollow Chronicle*. Her face grew tight again, and once more she drew in and let out a few deep breaths. Then she headed in, figuring if she waited until she was completely mellow, she'd be older than Bertie and Cornelia.

The first time Jillian had been in the *Chronicle* office, she'd been on a field trip in middle school. One story tall and two blocks off the square, the building looked unchanged—ugly and windowless, except for a large one facing the street. Once she stepped inside, the odor of newsprint and machine oil met her immediately, along with the sounds of machinery in the back. A lackluster Boston fern with sunburnt fronds struggled for life in the window. The cement floor was dusty. She got a hint of déjà vu. The place seemed frozen in time.

Stacks of newspapers were piled on the counter of a reception desk, but there was no one behind it. In fact, it looked as if the entire enterprise had been deserted.

"Hello?" she called out. No one replied or came out of the back to greet her. This business of no one being where they should be irritated her even more. "Hello!"

Something out of sight crashed and clattered, someone growled something, and then a burly man with a shock of black hair, thick beard, and overalls over a white T-shirt came through a doorway. His scowl could curdle milk. Muttering and swearing, he wiped his hands on a rag and reached for an old wall phone without even noticing Jillian.

"Excuse me."

He jumped and fumbled with the receiver, nearly dropping it. He glowered at her for a few seconds, then shook his head as if chasing away unwanted thoughts. His face cleared and softened.

"Howdy, Jillian. I didn't see you standing there. How you been?"

"Hi, Alf. I'm here to see your brother-in-law. Could you get him for me?"

"I wish I could. I think I just broke the press." He looked over his shoulder toward the back.

"What do you mean you wish you could? Isn't he here?"

"He's in Oregon. He's got a sick relative out there."

"Oregon? Since when?"

"He left Tuesday. Asked me to look after things here, but—" He shook his head.

"What do you know about this?" She slapped the crumpled newspaper on the counter and gouged the story about the bakery with her index finger.

He glanced at it. "That's the story about your granny and her business. I'm sure—"

"Where did it come from? Did Rod write it? Did you? Where did you get your facts? Why didn't someone come to The Chocolate Shoppe or the house and talk to Bertie first?"

He leaned back and blinked as if she had kicked sand in his face. "Hey, hey! Slow down, there."

She held up both hands, a gesture of cooperation, and forced herself to speak calmly. "Who is responsible for this piece, you or Rod?"

"I am. I mean, I'm responsible for this entire week's newspaper because Rod got called away all of a sudden."

"So you wrote this?" Her gaze pinned him like a dead bug in a science fair exhibit.

"Mostly. I took the original piece that came in and did some editing—"

"What do you mean 'the original piece that came in'?"

"The copy that came through the letter box. I reckon Rod gets most of his community items that way. They're mostly written or typed, then dropped there." He pointed at the door where a basket caught letters dropped through the mail slot. "Or they bring them inside, if we're open."

"But this piece of 'news' came in through the mail slot?"

"Yup."

"Who wrote it?"

"I don't know."

"There wasn't a signature?"

"Nope. I can show it to you." He opened the top drawer of a filing cabinet and pulled out a file folder. "Here." He slid the page of single-spaced typing across the counter to her.

She read it. "You pretty much changed nothing."

"Well, I did change 'they're' to 'there.'" He tapped the line with the error.

"But you used this, and it had no signature, so you don't know where it came from."

"Right."

"But you didn't double-check the facts in this anonymous article."

His face reddened. "When I'm here all alone, there's not much time for that. But you're right. I guess I should've done that."

"Yes, you should've. I believe any newspaper person knows that."

He looked somewhere between peeved and ashamed. "I'm a tree farmer, not a newspaper person. I just help Rod in a pinch."

"This time the pinch has hurt someone. My grandmother. And me. And everyone else connected with The Chocolate Shoppe."

"I'm sorry, Jillian. You know I'd never intentionally do anything to hurt any of you. You know that."

Out of his element, doing his best, he had zigged when he should have zagged. She reluctantly understood.

"What's done is done." She took a deep breath and let it out slowly so she wouldn't bite his head off. "Here's the thing: If you can't tell me who wrote this, I want you to run a retraction." She waved the typed page.

He shrugged. "I don't know. I'm sorry. I don't have time to write stuff, but if you want to write some kind of rebuttal, I guess I could—"

"Oh, good grief! Never mind. Do you have a list of correspondents who contribute regularly?"

He glanced around helplessly, as if he thought an amateur reporter would materialize out of the dust and clutter.

"Um. Yeah. Maybe."

An acrid odor that had been absent earlier tickled Jillian's nose. "What is that smell? Is something burning back there?"

He lifted his nose like a hound in the wind. "Aw, man! Sorry, Jillian." He ran to the back room.

When it became apparent from the noise and clatter that the machine needed intervention, she figured Alf would not be returning any time soon. Then she realized that even if she knew who had submitted the piece, there was no reason to talk to them directly. There had been only two others in the bakery who had been present during the discussion with Grant Bower, and they had blatantly eavesdropped, hanging on every word. She hated the very thought, did not want to believe it. She had hoped she'd learn differently here at the *Chronicle* office.

But the truth is the truth, and that's all there is to it.

Pulling into Maudie Honeycutt's driveway a few minutes later, Jillian was unsurprised to see Wanda Jean's car. The two women had been best friends since they were toddlers and were nearly as close as Bertie and Cornelia. They seldom bickered, and she wondered if they kept their squabbles private.

Laughter came through the open windows of Maudie's

bungalow. Grace, an aging shar-pei, pressed her nose against the screen door. Mosey, one of Maudie's two basset hounds, stood next to her and eyed Jillian sorrowfully. Sorrowful was his constant expression, even when his tail was wagging happily as it was right then.

Hugh Honeycutt—Maudie's friendly, white-haired husband—came to the door before Jillian knocked.

"I could tell by the enthusiastic greeting that someone we know and like was at the door," he greeted. He pushed the door open. "Good morning, Jillian. Come on in."

"You call this enthusiastic?" She petted both canine heads. "They are extremely polite."

"Hey, they got up off their beds and went to the door. That's enthusiasm in this house." He watched her scratch the dogs' ears. "How's Miss Bertie and Miss Cornelia?"

Jillian straightened and turned from the dogs.

"That's why I'm here. I need to talk with Maudie and Wanda Jean."

"The way it's grown quiet in that sewing room, I'm sure they know you're here and are listening to every word."

"That's no way to talk about us, Hugh." Maudie stepped into view with Wanda Jean right behind her. "What's wrong, Jillian?"

Looking at their concerned faces, one might have a hard time believing they'd caused so much harm. Deceitful people could be good at covering up and looking innocent. She reminded herself to be calm.

"Which one of you is responsible for the story in today's paper?"

They blinked at her.

"What story?" Maudie asked.

"Which paper?"

The squeak in Wanda Jean's voice underscored Jillian's suspicions. She pinned a hard look on the woman.

"What do you know about it, Wanda Jean?"

"I don't know anything. I haven't seen a newspaper since last week's *Moss Hollow Chronicle*."

"If you're talking about the local paper," Hugh said, "we haven't got this week's edition yet."

She never took her gaze off the two women. "It doesn't matter if you've got your copy or not, not if you're the ones who wrote that awful story."

Wanda Jean and Maudie looked completely bewildered. So much so that Jillian's certainty wavered.

"We don't have the least idea of what you're talking about, so why don't you fill us in?" Maudie suggested.

"One moment, please." Jillian stalked out of the house and got her paper out of the car. When she returned, she thrust it at them and tapped the article so hard the paper tore. "This right here. This is what I'm talking about."

Hugh laid one hand lightly on her shoulder. "Don't get so riled, child. Let us read what you're talking about."

Maudie smoothed the paper and read the article aloud. She raised a stricken look to Jillian. "We didn't tell any of this to Rod. None of it."

Wanda Jean shook her head, staring at the page.

"You two were the only ones in the bakery at the time Grant Bower talked with us."

"So what? We didn't talk to Rod."

"That piece was typed up and dropped into the mail slot. I saw it. It wasn't signed."

"I don't have a typewriter," Wanda Jean said.

"Neither do I." Maudie shoved the newspaper back at Jillian. "And we weren't the only ones in that place. Lenora was right there listening to every word."

"That's right." Wanda Jean nodded so hard her glasses slid down her nose.

Jillian's mouth flew open at the very notion. "I can't believe you said that. Lenora would never do something like that. She is neither a gossip nor a troublemaker."

"Neither are we!" Maudie drew herself up to her full height.

"I resent the implication." Wanda Jean sniffed and turned her face, as if the very sight of Jillian offended her.

Jillian felt torn, half of her clinging to the belief these two were responsible for the story, the other half sure they would never hurt her grandmother in this way.

"Someone, somewhere, said something to the wrong person."

"I don't know how many ways I can tell you, Jillian." Maudie's voice was hard. "*We* are not responsible for that story, but if you don't know us any better than that and hold us in such low regard, then you can just leave." She made a shooing motion with one hand. "Go back to the bakery, or Belle Haven, or wherever you want."

"And you can tell your grandmother not to expect us at any of the Sweetie Pies meetings from here on out," Wanda Jean added. "At least not if they're being held at The Chocolate Shoppe."

"That's right," Maudie agreed.

The words that tried to escape from her lips were words Jillian refused to speak aloud.

"Fine," she snapped. "But I *will* get to the bottom of this."

Maudie grabbed Wanda Jean's arm and pulled her out of sight and back into the sewing room.

Hugh walked Jillian to the door. He was as courteous and kindly as ever, but his smile failed to reach his eyes.

"Maudie would never intentionally hurt anyone, Jillian. You know that."

She swallowed hard. "I've always believed so, but someone did, and you know as well as I do that as good-hearted as they are, those two women in there like to run their mouths."

Hugh's friendly regard changed, and he opened the door. "I suggest you look elsewhere for the person responsible for that story."

"Believe me, this isn't over, not by a long shot. I won't stop until I find out who's behind it and why."

12

Jillian dreaded telling Bertie what had transpired at Maudie's house. Ever since the first rumor of the new bakery surfaced, it seemed that all she'd done was to deliver bad news of one sort or another to her grandmother.

She parked in the front lot of the bakery, and with a sinking heart, noted the only car in the parking lot was Stewie Franks's old red pickup. She rested her head against the steering wheel for a moment, imagining her grandmother's reaction when she found out Jillian had just estranged two of the most loyal members of the Southern Sweetie Pies.

I'm not telling her anything. At least not right now.

"So is Rod going to print a retraction next week?" Bertie said the moment Jillian walked into the bakery.

"Rod's in Oregon with a sick relative."

Bertie drew in a sudden breath. "Not Donnie."

"Donnie?"

"His cousin, Donnie Poole. He left Moss Hollow the minute he graduated high school. Such a nice boy, bless him. Is he all right?"

"I don't know. Alf didn't say."

Bertie frowned, and Lenora stopped sweeping the already clean floor to come stand beside her.

"Are you telling me Alf Rinkle is minding the press?" Lenora asked.

"Rod had to leave suddenly, and Alf stepped in."

"He's no newspaperman."

Jillian couldn't help but smile a little at that. "He knows that. In fact, he was wrangling with something in the back that made a lot of noise and plenty of stink."

"Maybe the press will break and we won't have any more foolishness out of it." Lenora stalked away, shaking her head and muttering.

Bertie stared out the window at the passing traffic, but Jillian could tell she wasn't watching the cars.

"Poor Donnie. I hope he's all right. He had polio when he was little, you know." She glanced at Jillian, who shook her head.

"I didn't know, but I'm sorry to hear that."

"Bad, bad time," Bertie said, her eyes fixed once more on a point outside. "Polio struck the young ones, mostly."

Lost in her thoughts, she didn't notice when Jillian slipped away to the back room where Lenora was putting away the broom. She filled Lenora in on the morning's events.

"What shall I say to her? I mean, the last thing she needs right now is to lose friends."

Lenora pressed her lips together and shook her head, a frown puckering her brow. "Mm-mm-mm. That is plenty troublesome. And you know word will get around to Bertie soon."

"I know. I feel just *awful*."

"Sure you do. That's because you're a good girl who cares about folks." Lenora patted her arm. "I tell you what. I'll break it to her. She'll likely take it better from me."

"Oh, but—"

"I'll pick the right time, honey. I won't just spring it on her." The bell above the door tinkled. "There goes our third customer of the day."

The sound of several voices caught their attention.

"Sounds to me more like someone has come, not gone. Several someones, in fact." Jillian led the way to the front.

Savannah and four other smiling women greeted her and Lenora. Behind them marched Hunter and several men, all dressed in business suits. Bertie looked brighter than she had in several days.

"I'm here for a dozen raised and a dozen cake," Laura Lee Zane said. "We deputies need our energy, you know."

"That you do," Lenora said with a grin as she reached for a box.

"And I need six bear claws and eight cream-filled Long Johns," Savannah said.

"I'll get those for you, honey," Bertie said.

"And we're here for a short business meeting," said Hunter. "Is it all right if we take over those two tables by the coffee station, Bertie?" He looked at Jillian and his warm smile almost melted her heart. "Oh, and we'll need coffee all around and bring out a platter loaded with those pecan sticky rolls you have made so famous."

Jillian watched the two women happily fill orders, tears swimming in her eyes. Savannah edged up to her and slipped an arm around her shoulders.

She gave Jillian a warm squeeze and whispered, "We're not going to let this bakery close. I promise."

Hunter sidled up on the other side of Jillian and wrapped his arm around her shoulders. "That goes double for me, Jillian. You can count on Savannah—and me."

Jillian and Bertie had been home only a few minutes that evening when a visitor knocked on the door.

"Who now?" Bertie grumbled. "Can't people leave folks alone after work?"

"Mercy sakes," Cornelia said, giving her a look of reproach. "I'll get the door, and whoever it is, we need to be neighborly."

Bertie rubbed her temples. "I'll try."

The day had gone better at the bakery thanks to their friends, but customers and sales were still fewer than usual, and Jillian had watched as her grandmother's hopeful mood dwindled.

Before closing, Lenora had pulled Bertie aside and gently told her about Maudie and Wanda Jean. Bertie accepted the news with a sigh and shrug. She said nothing at all about the situation to Jillian, and Jillian didn't know if that was a good thing or not. Rather than poke at a sore spot, she, too, decided to let sleeping dogs lie.

"Shall I get you some aspirin?" Jillian asked. When Bertie nodded, she hurried to the bathroom medicine cabinet. She wished she had the power to banish the last two months. She wished she had the money to whisk the two old dears to some exotic, quiet, and peaceful location, where they could rest and relax. Unable to do either one, the least she could do was to tend to their needs.

When she returned to the sitting room with a glass of water and the aspirin bottle, she found a thin, dark-haired man in a dark-blue suit, sitting on the edge of the sofa. He talked so quickly his words seemed tangled. He stopped speaking and stood up when Jillian approached.

"Ah, you must be the granddaughter. Julie?" His thin face was flushed, and he held out a well-manicured hand.

"Jillian," all three women corrected.

She handed Bertie the water and the aspirin, then shook his hand.

"Yes, yes, of course. *Jillian.* I'm Tim Naylor, a listing agent with Preferred Prime Properties, Inc. We've just opened our Moss Hollow office. I'm hoping—"

"He wants to buy The Chocolate Shoppe," Cornelia interrupted. The expression on her face very plainly proved what she thought of the idea.

"No, no," he said with a little laugh, lifting one hand. "That's not quite what I said. I—"

"Yes, it is," Bertie said.

"No, no." He turned to Jillian. His next words poured from his lips so fast no one could interrupt. "What I said was that even before the article came out in today's paper, the scuttlebutt in town was that the bakery might be up for sale. Now, I've heard you're thinking of renovation and expansion, but selling is your better option. I've also heard that the town is finally trying to catch up with the rest of the country. Moss Hollow businesses are moving away from the tired old downtown of the past, and into the busier, more affluent areas that spread outward, as evidenced by Confections & Donuts." He leaned forward, his face a mask of earnest entreaty. "Now is the time to sell before downtown property values drop even more. I'm the man for the job. I'm confident I can get it sold before the end of the month, and in fact, I already have had a couple of nibbles—"

"Why would you have nibbles when we haven't listed it? We aren't even sure we want to." Bertie shot a glance at Jillian.

"Now, Mrs. Harper, if you'll just take a look at what I have here. I brought paper because I know people of your generation don't care for digital technology." He reached for his leather attaché case, but Jillian got ahold of it before he could and she held it firmly.

"Thank you for your interest, Mr. Naylor. If we need you, we'll call you."

He blinked at the case in her hand. "But—"

"I'll show you to the door."

He got to his feet, slowly, his expression one of wounded feelings. Jillian figured someone with a softer head might fall for that look, but she treated it as the ploy it was.

"If you want to keep a bakery," he said, "I can find you a bigger, better location on the outskirts of town. It might be a little pricey, but it will bring in more business and will pay for itself in a few years. In fact, I know just the place—"

"This way, please." She forced a polite smile and gestured to the way out.

"I'll leave this for you to look over." He pulled a colorful brochure from the inner pocket of his jacket. When no one took it, he laid it on the coffee table. "And I'll stay in touch, in case you change your minds."

"We won't. This way, Mr. Naylor." Jillian waited until he was out the front door before handing him his briefcase. "Good evening." She closed the door firmly, then locked it just in case he felt the need to come back inside and add more to his pitch.

When she turned, Bertie and Cornelia stood a few feet away, grinning at her.

"Good job, honey. He didn't seem to want to listen to us," Bertie said.

"We told him 'no' about a dozen times," said Cornelia, "but he acted like we were dumber than a box of rocks."

"Even if I decide to sell," said Bertie, "he'd be the last one I'd sign with. He's pushy, and I don't trust him."

"I never heard anyone talk so much and say so little," Cornelia said.

"Then you've never met Leslie Phipps," said Jillian. "The two of them ought to get together."

"I'm getting strong vibrations from Raymond." Cornelia held up one finger as if asking for silence from a crowd. "He's telling us to be wary."

"We don't need Uncle Raymond to tell us that. Common sense speaks pretty loudly." Jillian looked toward the kitchen. "Have you started supper?"

"Not yet. I'm going to go freshen up a little first. He made me feel like I'd been closed up in a hot room." Bertie took a couple of steps, then paused. "Leslie Phipps. Isn't she that odd little thing you went to school with?"

"Yes. She volunteers at the chamber office."

Cornelia flung out one hand as if chasing away flies. "Don't mention that office to either of us. Or real estate agents. Come on, honey. Let's get supper going while Bertie rests a little."

"I'm not resting. I'm freshening up."

"Whatever."

"Aunt Cornelia, you sound like a teenager."

"Do I look like one too?" She struck a pose.

"Exactly," said Jillian.

At the same time, Bertie said, "Of all the ridiculous—"

Jillian and Cornelia giggled as they went to the kitchen.

"At least we had more than just us at the Sweetie Pies meeting yesterday," Jillian said Monday morning as she restocked the supply of sugar, sweetener, and creamer at the coffee station.

"A handful is still a handful." Bertie tipped her head to one side and eyed the display of doughnuts. "Confections & Donuts has two-for-the-price of one on Mondays. I reckon I can have a special on Tuesday. Buy two day-olds, get one free."

"Hush that kind of talk." Lenora put her hands on her hips. "We've had more customers today than we had by this time on Saturday."

"That's right." Jillian crushed the empty box that had held plastic stirrers. "Business is picking back up."

"We'll be back to our usual jump-and-run-around pace here soon enough."

Bertie huffed. "I tell you what. All that talk after church yesterday about Confections & Donuts, going on and on about their cream-cheese tartlets and black-bottom cherry snaps wore me out. And then someone asked me if The Chocolate Shoppe would still be open for business in a month."

"Forget that," Jillian said. "You have a few tricks up your sleeves, Bertie. You and Lenora both. Come up with some new treats and run a special on them."

"Good idea, Jillian." Lenora beamed at her.

Bertie chewed her lower lip, eyes narrowed, gaze fixed. If she'd heard Jillian's suggestion, she failed to show it. "I've been thinking. Maybe now would be a good time for you to go visit your daughter, Lenora. You could take as many days—"

"I'm not going anywhere, so don't be bringing that subject up again."

The door opened and Stewie Franks came in. "Mornin'." He got a large coffee and two doughnuts.

Jillian met Lenora's eyes as he paid. Lenora wriggled her eyebrows and grinned. This was the first time Jillian could remember the old man getting anything other than a small coffee and one doughnut.

"How are you today, Stewie?" she asked.

"Middlin'." He glanced around, spotted the Atlanta newspaper, grabbed it and settled in his usual place in the corner.

"Good sign." Jillian smiled at Bertie.

"Maybe he was extra hungry."

"Maybe business is picking up."

Customers came in modest numbers, and nearly all of them asked if the bakery was really going out of business.

"Not if we can help it," Jillian and Lenora said over and over.

Bertie simply said, "I have no comment."

The barber, Rome Hampstead, stopped by and bought a selection of assorted cookies. "I decided to offer my customers a free cup of coffee and a cookie. Every day. I'll make the coffee, but I'm getting my baked goods right here from y'all."

Jillian wanted to hug him and might have done so if she thought he wouldn't be embarrassed.

"I hear the new bakery has a special every day," Matt Harris said when he came in a bit later. "Y'all gonna do that?"

"Don't you think The Chocolate Shoppe is fine just the way it is?" Jillian asked.

"It's fine with me. I like the atmosphere here, and the friendly hometown bakers." His grin included all of them. "Over there at that new place, I feel like I'm sittin' in a little girl's dollhouse. Spindly chairs and pink froufrou everywhere. Plus, the staff isn't allowed to chat with customers. Those two gals that run the place look like they've been sucking lemons and sour pickles."

"So we aren't losing your business?"

"Miss Lenora, the only way you can lose my business is to tell me to get lost and never come back."

The bell above the door rang, and a man Jillian had never seen before walked in. She caught her breath and felt her eyes go big. Tall, golden-haired, and muscular in a spotless white Oxford shirt and well-fitting jeans, he was easily the best-looking man she had ever seen. He glanced around and stirred her heart even more when he met her gaze and offered a warm, intimate smile, as if they shared a secret.

Matt cleared his throat, hiding a grin behind his hand. "Say, Jillian, could I have a refill on this coffee?"

"Huh?" She blinked and looked at him. He held up his cup, eyes dancing. "Oh, sure. Yeah. Of course."

It wasn't until she'd replaced the pot on the warmer that she realized what had happened. Most of the customers helped themselves to the coffee, especially the regulars. Especially when they sat next to the coffee station as Matt did.

"Ha, ha," she said to him in an undertone. "Very funny."

"I've heard of being starstruck before, but wow." He shook his head, still grinning.

"A star?" She looked at the stranger who now perused the display of baked goods.

Matt shrugged. "Looks like one, but I don't think he is. Most stars don't drive ten-year-old cars with faded paint."

She followed his gaze to an older model sedan with the color and shine of dried mud.

"Guess not." Once again she looked at the stranger, admiring the style of his thick, pale hair, his handsome features, the gleam of his leather shoes. He was chatting with Bertie and Lenora, both of whom wore big smiles. In fact, Bertie's eyes hadn't sparkled like that in a long time. Without a moment's thought, Jillian left the coffee station and strolled behind the counter to listen.

"Good morning," he said to Jillian. "I was just telling these sweet ladies how enticing everything looks." His chocolate-brown eyes gazed into hers a few moments longer than necessary, then he ran his gaze along the pastries. "I can't decide what I want, so would you please give me one of everything?"

"Everything?"

"Yes. No, wait. I'll have two of those." He pointed to the sugar cookies. "I have to admit to being a sucker for sweets."

Jillian felt giddy and silly as she boxed up his order.

Yes, he's handsome, but so what? So is Hunter. So are a lot of men. And yes, he seems interested in me, but he's just being friendly. He's friendly to Bertie and Lenora as well. He's probably a very friendly person.

Still, her fingers were a little tingly when he paid.

"I'm Rick Drummond. And you are?"

"Jillian Green. The owner's granddaughter."

He glanced at Bertie, who was watching them "So you two are related?"

"That's right," Jillian said.

"I see where you get your good looks. Your grandmother is a beautiful woman."

"Yes, she is." She counted back his change and wished he would not gaze at her so intently. It was like he could see into her soul. "Thank you and come again."

"I'm coming back for sure. Soon." He smiled, turned to include Lenora and Bertie. "Have a good day, ladies."

As soon as he left, Lenora began fanning herself with both hands. "Mercy me. I need to sit."

"Why, Lenora!" Bertie said as the woman plopped down in the nearest chair. "He's young enough to be your son."

"Maybe so, but he's not. Did you ever see such a smile?"

"Not in a long time. He said his name was Rick Drummond? That doesn't ring a bell, but I feel like I know him from somewhere."

Lenora flapped one hand. "That's because he looks like a cross between Gregory Peck and Gary Cooper."

"Pfft. You're absurd." Bertie turned to Jillian who remained behind the cash register, gazing out the window as the old sedan drove away. "No need to ask what *you* thought of him."

"She's starstruck," Matt said, guffawing.

Jillian snapped her attention back into the bakery. "I most certainly am not."

"You looked like your eyes were about to fall out of your head."

"Matt Harris, you hush now." Bertie frowned at him. "There's nothing wrong with looking at a handsome fella."

"Not as long as you pick your eyeballs up off the floor when he's gone."

Jillian's face was so hot she hurried to the restroom, away from the laughter. Had Rick Drummond actually seemed interested in her or was he just friendly and she had misinterpreted his dark gaze? Had she ogled and goggled him like a silly schoolgirl the way Matt had implied with his teasing, or had she been properly mature as befitted a woman reaching her middle years?

There's no reason even to speculate. Hunter and I have a good friendship, and I won't muddy those still waters. She splashed cool water on her face, then met her own gaze in the mirror. *Maybe I'll call Hunter to see if he wants to go to a movie.*

But she didn't.

Trrue to his word, Rick Drummond returned to The Chocolate Shoppe several times. He always bought quite a few pastries to take with him.

"He's going to get fat as a butterball if he doesn't watch out," Lenora said.

"He probably runs every day or works out at the gym," Jillian replied.

"Maybe he takes those extras home to his family."

"Maybe." Jillian had wondered if he had a wife and kids, but he'd never mentioned anyone at home. He didn't wear a wedding ring. "Could be he takes the extras to his coworkers."

Rick's easygoing manner, friendly smile, and genuine interest in others made him a welcome customer and quickly earned him friends. One morning he gave Jillian a twenty-dollar bill as he left, and asked her to pay for as many purchases as the money would cover.

"If they ask who paid for it, just tell them a friend," he added.

"I believe that's the first time someone has done that," Bertie said.

Jillian sighed. "He is really nice." She blushed when she heard herself and picked up the window cleaner to polish the glass of the display case.

"I wonder what he does for a living," Bertie said. "He always shows up nicely dressed, every hair in place, clean-shaven. He gives the impression of a hardworking man who's comfortably well-off, but that old car he drives doesn't look like the kind of car a well-to-do businessman would own. Do you know, Jillian?"

"He told me his life's work is a mission of helping people. He drove through Moss Hollow and felt compelled to stay for a while, maybe even settle here."

"But how does he earn his living?"

"He has some investments in Memphis and St. Louis. Real estate and that sort of thing. They seem to be doing quite well, but he did mention he misses working with his hands."

"I see. It's noble of him to want to help others. For his sake, I hope those investments keep producing income."

Savannah called Wednesday evening. "Have you heard anything about Gordon Brett?"

"Nothing," Jillian replied. "I drive over to his place every day, but he's never home."

"Are you sure he's not simply avoiding you?"

"Weeds are growing in his vegetable beds, so I don't think so. I think he's disappeared."

"Goodness. Have you talked with the sheriff?"

"I called him. He said he was keeping an eye out and I needn't concern myself. You know Coy Henderson is not going to utter one syllable to me or anyone else if he doesn't have to. I couldn't get anything more out of him."

Savannah sighed. "Gordon might have created this situation for himself, but I hope he's all right."

"So do I."

"By the way, you aren't seriously interested in this Rick Drummond guy, are you?"

"What? Why would you ask that?"

"Because you have a certain trio of women concerned. And now I'm wondering too."

Jillian pushed out an exasperated sigh. "There is nothing to be concerned about. Rick is good-looking, charming, and kind. I enjoy chatting with him. But that's it."

"You're sure?"

"One hundred percent. Bertie, Aunt Cornelia, and Lenora—and you—have nothing to worry about. What's the deal, anyway? I thought everyone wanted to see me settled."

"It's just that no one knows him yet. I want you to be careful."

"I always am."

She chose to ignore Savannah's snort.

Business continued to pick up that week. Several regulars returned, and some of them confided to Jillian they had given the new bakery a try, but it was too impersonal and the food tasted more like packaged supermarket fare than freshly baked products.

"See, Bertie?" she said. "The lull in business was temporary while folks sampled something new. We have loyal fans, and Confections & Donuts could never steal them away, no matter how many specials they have or how much they advertise."

Some of Bertie's tension eased, but she continued to worry. Her appetite remained minimal, and Jillian's concern lingered.

"Are you still thinking about having the addition built?" she asked as Bertie stood beside the counter, arms folded, looking toward the back.

"Yes, I am. We might not be in danger of losing the business, but I think making the shop bigger and offering more variety would be a good step to increasing revenue. And one of these days, Jillian, when you take over, you'll be glad of it."

An uneasy shiver shot down her spine as she thought of that last statement. "One of these days" in that context meant Bertie would no longer be running The Chocolate Shoppe, and

the only reason for that would be if she were too infirm or—
Jillian shoved the thought from her mind unfinished.

"Say, Bertie," Stewie hollered. It was Friday morning, and he
was looking at her over the top of the *Moss Hollow Chronicle*.
The paper from Atlanta lay neatly beside his plate, unopened
and unread. "Did you see this?" He flicked his finger against
something in the paper, then reinserted his hearing aid so he
could hear her response.

"Is that last week's? Because, if it is, I have seen everything in
it I care to see. If it wasn't that I want to know what's going on in
my town, I'd cancel my subscription to that thing."

"You oughta anyhow," Lenora said.

"Now, ladies," Jillian said, "let's remember that last week's
paper was not Rod's fault. Not directly."

"No, it wasn't," Bertie replied. "But Alf should've known better."

"Rod should have known better than to leave that man in
charge, even for a week," Lenora said. "I could've done better."

"Lenora, you don't know the first thing about newspapers,"
Jillian countered.

"Neither does Alf Rinkle."

"What're you referring to, Stewie?" Bertie asked. "No, don't get
up to show me. I'll come to you. More coffee?" Without waiting
for a reply, she carried the pot to his table and filled the cup, then
sat down to look at whatever had caught his interest.

"I don't feel good about this," Lenora said in an undertone.

"Me either."

"Yep. Look at her face. Bad news."

Hard lines settled between Bertie's eyebrows, and her cheeks went pink.

"*Oh!*" She sounded like someone had punched her. She folded the paper into a square and held it close to her face as if proximity would change whatever she had found there, then glared at Stewie. "Who in the world is Jimmie-June Jessup?"

"Who?" Jillian and Lenora said in unison.

Stewie reared back. "Don't look at me like that. I just found the piece, I didn't write it or print it. And obviously I don't agree with it. If I did, I'd be somewheres else."

Bertie lowered her head, sighing loudly. "I know that, Stewie, and I appreciate it." She shook her head.

"Let's see what you're talking about. May I have the paper, Bertie?" Jillian crossed the room and took the newspaper from her grandmother's slack hand.

"I reckon I shouldn't have said anything." Stewie looked miserable.

Bertie patted his arm. "Piffle. I would have seen it sooner or later."

Lenora stood next to Jillian as they read:

Dear Editor,

As a longtime resident of the area, I feel I should be completely honest. The recent arrival of Confections & Donuts to our town proves we residents of Moss Hollow are ready to embrace progress in the form of newer, larger, more budget-friendly businesses. The corporations in our country provide job security, while "mom-and-pop" businesses keep money in their own pockets by employing only family. Offering no choice to consumers ensures the cycle of small-town economics—i.e., unemployment, poverty-level income, dependence on government programs—will

*continue. Case in point is The Chocolate Shoppe, a bakery
owned, operated, and staffed by one family. Not only
are the baked goods frequently stale and unappetizing,
the staff is generally uncooperative and unfriendly. The
bakery itself isn't even clean. I, for one, am glad we have
an alternative bakery to enjoy, and look forward to other
new businesses now moving into our town.*

Sincerely,

Jimmie-June Jessup

Jillian looked up. "This Jessup woman says she's a longtime resident. So why don't any of us know her?"

"I would remember a name like that." Bertie pointed at the newspaper.

"Sounds made up, doesn't it?" Lenora stared hard at the article, as if doing so would change or reveal something.

"Maybe someone made it up so's no one would know who it is," Stewie inserted. "That's an ugly letter written about one of the nicest places and run by the best folks in town."

"Aw, Stewie." Jillian gave him a tender smile. "Thank you." She glanced at Lenora. "And it's official."

She raised one eyebrow. "What is?"

"You're family. You and Maggie both. Says so right there in that letter that only family works here."

Bertie nodded. "You'd better believe it."

Lenora's dark eyes flooded. "Thank you, honey. Family doesn't always mean blood, does it? Now, if you'll excuse me, I have something to do in the kitchen." She grabbed Jillian's hand. "You come help."

Jillian allowed herself to be pulled along, figuring the woman didn't want Bertie or Stewie to see her cry. But in the kitchen, she was dry-eyed.

"You reckon one of those two gossipy old gals wrote that letter to get even?"

"Who?"

"You know who."

Jillian winced. "You mean Maudie and Wanda Jean?"

"The very ones."

"I doubt it. They're not vindictive."

Lenora's frown deepened. "There's something not right about that letter, Jillian."

"I know that. And anyone who's been here will know it's a pack of lies."

"Yeah, but what we gotta figure out now is who wrote it, and why that newspaper printed such baloney."

A brief silence fell.

"I upset Alf Rinkler about this time last week," Jillian said. "I guess it's time to do it again."

"That's what I was thinking. You go shake him up. Get to the bottom of this mess. I'll look after your grandma."

"You got it."

An hour later, Jillian returned to The Chocolate Shoppe no closer to the truth and thoroughly disgusted.

"Alf said the letter was signed, and the rule is as long as there's a signature and no swear words, all letters to the editor are published on the editorial page."

"Even big fat lies about people?" Lenora eyes flashed.

"Yep. Then he said he thought he'd done a good deed by helping his brother-in-law and running the paper for him, but it had caused him enough aggravation to last a lifetime. He told me he had had it 'up to here,' and then he escorted me to the door, and more or less pushed me out. He locked the door, turned the sign to *Closed*, and stomped off."

"Forevermore," Bertie said. "What got into him?"

"Well, I knew he didn't have enough sense to run that newspaper," Lenora sniffed. "We all would've been better off if Rod had closed shop while he was gone."

Jillian decided not to mention that she'd driven past Confections & Donuts and had seen Maudie's car in the parking lot.

Sunday afternoon, several members attended the Sweetie Pies meeting, including two new and unexpected visitors. Carrying several pink-and-white polka-dot gift bags, they breezed in through the front door at exactly two o'clock, just after Bertie had welcomed everyone. Dressed in a pink linen sheath dress, Alyce Sherman bestowed a warm smile all around. Her sister, in dark-rose slacks and a sleeveless white blouse, ran a quick, friendly gaze across the group.

"Good afternoon, all!" she sang out. "We've heard so much about the Sweetie Pies that we decided to join you today."

"And we come bearing gifts!" Breanna added, brandishing her bounty.

"Who are you?" Annalise asked.

"I'm Breanna Sherman." She handed Annalise a package. "Alyce is my twin sister."

"Twins!" Cornelia exclaimed.

"That's right. I heard you and Mrs. Harper are twins as well. We have something in common besides owning bakeries, don't we?" Alyce gave her a smile and a package. "Inside these gift bags you will find a sample of treats available at Confections & Donuts."

She paused and glanced around. "This being a baking club, I do hope you all have checked out our bakery. It's not as . . . cozy as here in The Chocolate Shoppe."

"There are coupons in the gift bags too," Breanna said. "We hope we'll be seeing you soon."

"You're seeing us now." Lenora voice was cold enough to freeze hot lava.

"I saw you at church this morning, didn't I?" Annalise added in a similar tone.

"At the Moss Hollow Fellowship Church? You surely did. Quite a lovely service, and such friendly folks."

"Most folks in Moss Hollow are friendly," Jillian said.

The sisters sat down side by side near the front and angled their chairs so they could see the group.

"The library is very nice," Alyce said. "I was so glad to see they carry books by my favorite author."

"You have time to read?" Lenora said. "I'd think that big bakery would keep you jumping all the time."

Breanna's smile seemed forced. "We like to keep busy in both body and mind." She glanced at the others. "I hope you enjoy your gifts."

By the time everyone left the meeting, the Belle Haven women, including Savannah and Lenora, were tense and unhappy.

"Did you ever?" Cornelia said as she locked the front door when the last person left.

"They took over the entire meeting." Lenora scowled. "Bertie, you should've told them to hush their mouths. Or at least talked more about The Chocolate Shoppe."

"You did a good job of that, Lenora," she replied. "Promising I'd make my cinnamon-pecan rolls every Wednesday and announcing we were lowering the price of chocolate chip cookies. When did we decide to do that? While I was asleep?"

Lenora put the chairs and tables back in place. "That just slipped out. You ought to be glad rolls and cookies were the only things that slipped out, because what I was thinking wasn't fit to broadcast." She met Bertie's eyes. "All that uptown diva talk doesn't sit well in my world. Them joining every church, library, and club in town isn't exactly endearing, if you ask me."

"It's all business," Savannah said. "That's why they're joining so many organizations."

"That's exactly right," Jillian said. "I saw that a lot in the city. They're networking, looking for customers, not friends."

Bertie and Cornelia sniffed in derision.

"Lenora's ideas were good," she added.

"Did you see the smirk on the skinny one's face?"

"They're both skinny," Cornelia said.

Bertie scowled. "Like she thought sticky buns were pitiful. I'll show her pitiful."

Following through on Lenora's suggestion, Bertie lowered the price of chocolate chip cookies. Jillian made signs to put in the windows and near the counter, advertising the change and the Sticky Bun Special.

Thursday morning, four tables were filled with chatting, smiling customers. Two more stood at the register to pay and four queued at the counter, waiting to be served. Bertie and Jillian happily took care of their needs.

"Guess I'd better call Maggie to come in after all," Bertie said. "I gave her the day off. It was her idea because business was down so much."

"Don't get worked up, Bertie," Jillian cautioned. "Just give her a call. More than likely, she'll—"

Someone screamed, then others shouted. A mad scramble of movement and shouting voices overtook the cheerful sounds of fellowship.

"What on earth?" Jillian yelled.

A flash caught her eye, then another. Two huge brown rats scurried across the floor, one heading toward the customers, the other darting toward the coffee station.

The bakery erupted in chaos as customers fled. In less time than seemed possible, the place emptied of everyone expect Jillian, Bertie, and Lenora. And the rats.

"Revolting!" Lenora glared at the carcasses in traps a few hours later. "Never could abide rats. Nasty, disgusting things." She shuddered.

Abe Barlow, the beefy exterminator Jillian had called, deposited the dead bodies into a trash bag. "Don't worry, ma'am. We'll go through the place with a fine-tooth comb and get rid of any more we see."

"And what about the ones you don't see? If I go to bed tonight, will I be crawling under the covers with some nasty ol' long-tailed rodent?"

"I didn't find any access points where rats could have gotten into the place."

"And yet there they are." Bertie pointed to the trash bag.

He grimaced, stared at the dead rodents, and shifted from one foot to the other. "Miss Bertie, I don't think these came in from outside."

"Then where did they come from?"

"I think maybe someone brought them in and turned them loose."

"Mercy. Who'd do such a thing?" Lenora fanned her face with a paper napkin.

"That's not for Abe to find out," Bertie told her. "And you'll stay at Belle Haven tonight and for as long as you want."

"I never been one to be afraid of much, but rats are another story." She shuddered again. "I'll take you up on your invitation."

"I'll go over the place again, just to make sure," Abe said. He walked around the bakery peering at corners, doorways, and beneath the counter. "Have you ever had much trouble with rodents?"

Bertie shook her head emphatically. "Never have."

"We keep the place clean," Jillian added.

"You should know, Abe. You come here and inspect every year to see that we don't get pests."

"I've never seen so much as a dropping," Lenora declared. "If I had, Bertie would've known, and I would've been staying at her house."

Abe grinned. "Don't you worry. I'll take care of everything, including any cleanup that needs to be done."

Bertie closed the bakery early, and the three of them headed out to Belle Haven.

Friday morning there were even more problems at The Chocolate Shoppe. As she started cracking eggs for a recipe, Lenora found each one spoiled. The stench was so bad in the kitchen that Jillian had to prop open the back door.

"How'd that happen?" Lenora asked. "I bought fresh eggs Monday. They couldn't all go bad that soon, not when they were good yesterday."

When Matt Harris bit into a cream-filled Long John, he gagged and spat it out into a handful of napkins.

"The filling's sour," he said, grabbing his coffee. He drained it in one go.

"But that's impossible," Bertie said. "I made that filling last night, and it's been in the refrigerator ever since."

Matt got up, cast an eye across the display of baked goods and shook his head. "You better check the rest of them," he said as he left.

When Lenora and Bertie examined the pastries, all the cream-filled ones were bad. "I guess we should've taken a good look and a good sniff before we put them out," Lenora said.

"You had no reason to be suspicious," Jillian said. "You and Bertie have done everything the same way for years and years. Nothing has ever been spoiled before. Is the refrigerator broken?"

Lenora shook her head. "I was just in there. Cold as a frosted frog in there."

"What is going on here?" Bertie said. "I don't understand. Why is this happening to us?" Her face was pale and shoulders rounded in defeat. The haunted expression in her eyes made Jillian physically ill.

And Jillian wished she had an answer.

That evening, Cornelia verbalized what Jillian had been thinking. "It's sabotage, plain and simple. That big bakery has set out to ruin us, and they're doing it. Gordon Brett was right. Big business is trying to take over Moss Hollow. Where is he, anyway?" She looked around the kitchen as if she expected him to be standing nearby, sipping sweet tea.

"I don't know," Jillian said. *Maybe he's fled the county.*

Cornelia took meat loaf from the oven. "Well, somebody better do something before this family ends up in the poorhouse."

Jillian shot a look at her grandmother, who was mashing potatoes with all the enthusiasm of an automaton.

"Aunt Cornelia?" she murmured. The bright-blue eyes met hers. "Don't say things like that. Please?"

Cornelia bit her lower lip and looked stricken. She nodded.

The doorbell rang.

"Someone smelled your supper, Aunt Cornelia. Stay there, I'll get it."

Jillian nearly jumped when she opened the door and saw Rick Drummond in all his handsome glory on the doorstep.

"Oh . . . hello." Her voice sounded silly. She cleared her throat. "Hi, Rick. Won't you please come in?"

His dark eyes looked straight into hers as he stepped inside. He reached out, pushed back a lock of her red hair that had escaped its clip, and gave her a warm smile.

"Good evening, Jillian. You look cute."

Cute? With her hair straggling, her face damp with sweat, and still dressed in her work clothes? Maybe he needed glasses.

"I hope I haven't come at a bad time." He looked uncertain, even embarrassed. "I can return later, if that's better."

"Um, no, this is fine."

Lenora stepped out of the kitchen. "Why, it's Gregory Peck."

"Who?" Cornelia asked as she came out of the kitchen and saw their guest. "Well, my goodness. When did you step out of Hollywood?" She tipped her head to one side and gave him a coy smile.

Rick laughed and shook his index finger at her as if scolding. "You're teasing me, Bertie."

"Fooled you!" Cornelia sang out.

"This is my great-aunt, Cornelia Montgomery, Bertie's twin," Jillian said. "And this is Rick Drummond. He's new in town."

"Twins?" Rick said, running his gaze over Cornelia. "There are *two* of you? Then I'm more than delighted to be here."

Cornelia giggled, and Jillian blushed in embarrassment. "You're just in time for supper. Won't you join us?"

He took a step back. "Forgive me. I didn't realize—I'm so sorry."

"Don't be sorry," Bertie said as she joined them. She was

actually smiling for the first time since they got home. "We have plenty, and my sister makes a fine meat loaf. Please sit down with us."

Jillian found her normal voice and dignity. "Yes, please do. We're eating in the breakfast nook this evening."

Cornelia linked her arm with his left one as Bertie took the right, and they herded him toward the supper table.

At one point during the meal he looked up and caught Bertie studying him. "Something on your mind, ma'am?"

She shifted as if embarrassed for being caught staring. "Excuse me for being rude. It's just that you remind me of someone, but I don't know who."

"I hear that a lot. I have one of those faces." He chuckled.

They continued with dinner mixing small talk with Bertie and Cornelia's tales of Belle Haven in the days of their youth. Lenora added tales about her daughter, son-in-law, and grandson, and Jillian told of her summer with Bertie before her move to California. Jillian was amazed at how comfortable the group of women felt with this virtual stranger.

"Ladies," he said at the meal's end, "I don't know when I've had a better meal or spent time with nicer folks."

They accepted his praise with smiles and thanks.

"Coming to Moss Hollow has been one of the best decisions I've ever made. I believe I've found the hometown I've been searching for all my life."

"How wonderful!" Cornelia said.

His smile seemed to light up the room. Looking at it, Jillian nearly sighed aloud.

"Where are you from, Mr. Drummond?" Cornelia asked.

"Please call me Rick. I've lived all over the United States, but most recently I lived in Missouri."

"And what do you do for a living?"

"I have some investments that provide adequately for me, and I've developed a variety of skills, although I'm not tied down to one particular line of work. As the old saying goes, I'm a jack-of-all-trades, master of none. I serve wherever I'm needed."

"Like a missionary?" Cornelia was all smiles and eyelashes.

He chuckled. "A little like that, yes. Now that I've decided to stay in Moss Hollow, I will probably open my own little handyman business."

"I think that's a great idea," Jillian said. "You'll be independent, but busy, I'm sure."

"Things fall apart all the time," Cornelia added. "Why, Belle Haven alone could keep you busy for a long time."

He beamed at her. "We'll have to talk about that after I've settled in." Bertie served coffee and vanilla-almond sponge cake, and when all had had their dessert, he continued. "While this dinner has been unexpected and delightful, I have a purpose in calling here this evening."

"I figured you did." Bertie put the coffeepot in place and sat down, linking her hands on top of the table. She looked at him expectantly. "What is it?"

"When I said earlier that I've found my hometown, I meant it. And The Chocolate Shoppe has been one of the top reasons I love Moss Hollow." He met Jillian's eyes over the rim of his coffee cup, and his gaze seemed to say something far more than his words. She shifted in her seat and looked away.

"What a lovely thing to say, isn't it, Bertie?" Cornelia fingered the small ruby brooch on her blouse. She glanced at her sister and her face fell. "Oh my goodness."

Tears streamed down Bertie's wrinkled cheeks.

"Bertie!" Jillian jumped up and went to kneel next her grandmother's chair. "Are you all right?"

"Did I say the wrong thing?" Rick looked frantic.

"No, not at all." Jillian gave him a quick, reassuring smile. "It's just that we've had a stressful time since Confections & Donuts came to town."

"Of course. I can see where that would cause you distress."

"It's not just that horrid place," Bertie sobbed. "It's all the rest that's been happening."

His face filled with concern. "Like what?"

"First it was tearing down Guy & Ginger's," Cornelia said. "Wrecking a landmark that can never be replaced, a place where many happy memories were made. Just gone." She snapped her fingers.

Bertie nodded, "Yes, yes."

Before either woman could launch into a long and painful list of all that had happened recently, Jillian gave him a succinct overview of events. Frown lines settled across his brow.

"That's terrible. Disgraceful, as a matter of fact. I've visited the other bakery and believe me when I tell you that their offerings come nowhere near yours, Bertie. Nowhere near."

She gave him a weak, watery smile. "Thank you for saying so, but the damage has been done, I'm afraid. Not only can we not compete with the variety they offer over there, our place has been sullied by ugly letters in the newspaper, and rumors, and spoiled food—" Her voice broke and tears flowed. "No one wants to eat where rodents have been running around. Customers are going to abandon us like rats from a sinking ship."

Rick reached across the small table and took one of her hands in both of his. "I'm so sorry, so very sorry, that you've had to go through this. It's completely unfair to have your world turned upside down by these strangers."

Bertie nodded and sniffled. He gazed at her tenderly, with obvious concern. She wiped her eyes with a paper napkin.

"You're a stranger too. You hardly know any of us at all, but you've been nothing but kind."

"I simply act the way decent people should act. Look how nice all of you have been to me."

"It's not hard to be nice to a nice customer like you, Rick."

He gave her a warm smile, released her hand, and stood. "Let me do some thinking about this situation. I'm not without contacts and resources. Could be I can help find a solution."

"My goodness," Lenora said, her voice faint.

All four stared at him. Although Jillian had no idea what he could or would do to help them, hope burgeoned in her heart.

"I won't say more until I know more." He looked at Jillian. "Would you walk with me out to my car, please?"

"Of course." She hoped he was going to share with her his ideas for helping, perhaps ask for her input or opinion.

"Don't stay out too late," Cornelia called after them.

Jillian's face burned, but she pretended she hadn't heard.

Outside, Rick paused on the front veranda and looked around. "This is a lovely home you have. Has Belle Haven been in your family for a long time?"

She nodded. "Built before the War Between the States by Captain Hoyt Belle."

"Lucky family."

"Do you come from a big family, Rick?"

"Average. A brother and sister. My grandmother lived with us until she passed away."

He took her arm and they went down the steps toward his car. He stopped a few steps away from the driver's door and turned Jillian to face him. He was so close she could feel the warmth coming from his chest.

"I'm sure you know by now that I really like you, Jillian."

"You do?"

"I *do*." He lifted her chin so that he could look into her eyes. "I believe the feeling is mutual, yes?"

"Oh, um . . ." The awkward situation disengaged her brain for a few moments, and she broke the gaze while seeking a response. "Well, I . . ." She cleared her throat. "That is, I find you attractive."

She ventured a glance at his face. He lifted one eyebrow. "Is that all?"

"No. I think you are extremely, um, good-looking."

A smile twitched at the corner of his mouth. "And?"

She cleared her throat again. "And very nice."

He tipped his head to one side, studying her face, obviously waiting for her say more.

"And I really appreciate that you've offered to try to help my grandmother and great—"

Without warning, he bent his head and kissed her warmly and fully on the lips, halting not only her words but her breath. She gathered her wits quickly and leaned away, pushing against his chest.

"Excuse me! Did I give you the impression I wanted you to kiss me?"

He blinked and looked completely flabbergasted. He let go of her and quickly stepped back.

"I'm so sorry. I thought—Jillian, I am so sorry."

"Why did you do that?"

He gestured helplessly and looked miserable. "There's been this chemistry between us ever since we met. Or have I just imagined it?"

Her face flamed and she turned from his intense gaze. "I find you attractive, so maybe it's not been completely in your imagination."

He nodded and took a step toward her, but she held up one hand.

"Rick . . . There's someone in my life, and I care for him very much."

"You never mentioned a husband. I don't see a ring on your finger."

"We're not married, but we care for each other."

"And it's serious?"

Is it? Were she and Hunter moving into the realm of *serious*? Before she answered Rick, she took a moment to think about the question. Hunter was a good, decent man who'd been there for her again and again after her move back to Moss Hollow. Since the encroachment of Confections & Donuts he had proved himself a true and loyal friend. *But is he more than just a friend?* And now she knew the answer to the question.

"Yes, it is serious, Rick. I like you, but that's it. I'm sorry if I sent you the wrong signals or in any way led you to believe there could be anything more between us."

His face cleared, and he gave her a wry smile. "I understand. That's not to say I'm happy about the situation, but I do believe your guy is one lucky man. You deserve all the happiness you can find."

She relaxed, glad that he wasn't angry or offended by her rejection. He looked a bit hurt, but she was sure the hurt would be short-lived. With his charm, his warmth, his ability to empathize, and his looks, true love would find him someday.

"You will still try to help Bertie, won't you?"

"I'll do my very best for those sweet little ladies." He held out one hand. "Jillian, thank you for supper. And thank you for not slapping me." They shook hands, and he added wistfully, "I wish things were different, but I accept what is."

She smiled awkwardly and stepped back. "Good night, Rick."

When she went into the house, both women looked at her expectantly.

"Got a date?" Cornelia asked.

The last thing Jillian wanted to discuss with them was the awkward encounter she'd just had.

"Yes, in fact, I do. With Hunter next Wednesday evening. We're going to the singing over at Apple Grove Church. Good night now."

She hurried upstairs to her room and called Hunter to double-check that date. And to hear his voice.

15

Once again, the Sweetie Pies meeting at The Chocolate Shoppe was sparsely attended Sunday afternoon.

"There's so few of us here," Bertie said, "there's no reason to have a meeting."

"I think we should go ahead, Bertie," said Annalise. Laura Lee nodded in agreement.

"This galls me," Cornelia said. "Our friends and neighbors have tested the limits of my patience, and I'm fixin' to snap."

"Who can blame them for not showing up?" Bertie gestured around her. "Rodents, spoiled goods, me acting like I should be carried out in a straitjacket. Yes, I know I've not been myself. They probably think I'm going to go nutty right here in front of them all." She threw up her hands and stalked toward the back. "I'm going home."

Monday morning, Bertie and Jillian arrived at the bakery and found a piece of copy paper with words printed in a big black font taped to the glass.

Health hazard. Baked rats with icing. Eat here at your own risk.

Bertie tore it off and crumpled it into a ball without speaking. She silently pitched it into the trash, then retreated into the restroom. After several minutes, Lenora pressed her ear to the door. She rapped on it a few times. "Hey, you okay in there?"

"I'm fine."

"You don't sound fine." She beckoned Jillian. "Tell her to come out of there."

Jillian knocked. "Bertie, are you sick?"

No answer.

"Bertie?"

The door opened and she glowered at them. "Why are you pounding on the door and hollering at me while I'm in the bathroom?"

Lenora made a big show of looking at her watch. "You've been in there for ten minutes."

"So? It's the only place I can go and have a think. Except when people pound on the door. Leave me alone. Please." She closed the door in their faces.

"I wish I'd seen that awful piece of paper first," Lenora said. "I would've ripped it into a thousand pieces and taken it out to the dumpster so she'd never know."

"You can't blame yourself for this." She linked her arm with Lenora's and led her away from the door. "When Bertie comes out, be your usual cheery self, but keep one eye on her."

"You going somewhere?"

Jillian got her purse from beneath the counter, then dug the crumpled page from the trash can. "Yep. I'm going to make a little business call."

"Where? What are you doing with that paper? Who are you going to see?"

"I'll tell you about it when I get back. Just keep an eye on Bertie, please."

She thought about calling, or even emailing, the Sherman sisters, but a face-to-face encounter would not only save time, it would ensure she'd get answers. Determination and anger locked around her stomach like an iron fist, and she thought she might be sick.

A little discomfort never stopped me before, and it's not going to stop me now.

She drove across town to Confections & Donuts and pulled into a parking lot that boasted few empty spots. It took a minute and some deep breaths before she was ready. As she entered, light instrumental music played in the background, and the shiny new bakery practically hummed with pink-tinted activity. The fragrance of sugar, spices, and coffee hung in the air like a tantalizing cloud. Large glass display cases gleamed, showing off everything from breakfast sandwiches and pastries to mounds of candies.

Customers were seated at each of the many tables, most of them laughing and chatting as they ate. Four servers—boasting pink uniforms, perky pink hats, ruffly white aprons, and fixed smiles—stood stiffly behind the counter, not speaking. Two young men in white slacks and pink shirts patrolled the area with coffeepots. They never stayed to chat with customers, but continued to move through the room.

One of the Sherman twins stood behind the cash register. Dressed in a sleeveless white blouse, she sparkled with pink jewelry on both ring fingers, left wrist, neck, and earlobes. She had fixed her gaze and her smile on Jillian before recognition dawned. Her warm façade cooled.

"Good morning, Ms. Green. Are you here to redeem your coupon?" She stretched out one perfectly manicured hand for it.

"No, I left it at home. I'm actually here to talk with you and your sister."

"I'm sorry, but we don't have time." She smiled at someone behind her and said, "Good morning, sir." He stepped around Jillian and handed her his ticket. The woman swiped his credit card through the machine and gave it back to him. "Thank you, and come again." She turned to Jillian. "As you can see, we're far too busy to visit."

Jillian glanced around. Beyond the servers, she saw the other twin, arms folded, her hard gaze pinned on them.

"You have staff to cover for you. If we could meet privately for a few minutes—"

"Impossible. Breanna and I have a business to run, as you can see."

Jillain shoved down an urge to stomp her foot. She took the crumpled sign out of her purse, smoothed it, and laid it on the counter.

"This was taped to our bakery's front door this morning."

Alyce barely glanced at it and lifted one shoulder.

"Do you know who might have put it there?"

"No. Why should I?"

"Someone is trying to ruin our business, and since we had no trouble before Confections & Donuts came to Moss Hollow, logic tells me you are somehow connected."

The green eyes flashed, and a frown drew her perfectly shaped eyebrows together.

"I resent that."

"And I resent that this bakery has sent my grandmother into mental and emotional decline."

"You can't blame Confections & Donuts for that. Your grandmother is an old woman."

Alyce turned her forced smile and attention to a woman waiting to pay. Breanna joined them. Seeing them side by side, the differences in their appearance were subtle, but evident. Breanna had a sprinkling of freckles across her nose and cheeks, and her red hair was a couple shades lighter than her sister's. Alyce had a small diamond nose piercing.

"What's the trouble?" Breanna said in an undertone.

"I simply came over here to talk to you and Alyce. It would—"

"Don't be daft. Why would we want to chat with someone who is trying to hurt our business?"

Jillian blinked. "What's that supposed to mean?"

"You know full well what it means. The phone calls, the letters, the threats we've received, telling us to close down or else."

"You have? When?"

"You know we have, and you know when."

Jillian shook her head. "No. I don't know anything about that."

Breanna and Alyce looked at each other. One smirked and the other rolled her eyes.

"Of course you do," Breanna said. "Admit it."

"I admit nothing, because neither I nor my grandmother or anyone at our bakery has done anything. We're too busy trying to keep our business afloat. *We* are the ones being sabotaged. We've had to deal with ugly letters to the editor insulting us and our food, rats being turned loose in our bakery, and a whole host of other problems."

"Please," Alyce said. "A large, successful franchise like ours has no reason for such petty nonsense. But a tiny, backwater bakery like The Chocolate Shoppe would have every motivation to cause trouble."

Jillian's fingers curled. "We have not said or done one bad thing to you since you moved here. *Ever.*"

"I find that hard to believe." Breanna pressed her lips in a thin line. They stared at one another for a few moments.

"We've never had this kind of trouble before Confections & Donuts came to town."

"We own two other C&D shops, but Moss Hollow has been the first place where we've met resistance. Especially dark resistance." She glanced at her sister and took a step closer to her as if seeking strength and comfort. Jillian had seen Bertie and Cornelia do this during times of unrest. "We don't feel safe here. We think someone has even been inside our house."

"That's frightening."

"Yes it is."

"Did you call the police?"

"We aren't sure it happened, and we can't prove anything."

"But you could at least have the police on the lookout for suspicious activity."

Both women shook their heads. They looked genuinely upset. Was it possible that no one associated with Confections & Donuts had been responsible for recent events?

"We've had nothing like that at Belle Haven, but my best friend and I thought we saw someone watching my house one night. If we are having somewhat similar concerns at both bakeries," Jillian said, "then maybe—"

"Maybe someone has a reason to try to shut us both down." Breanna looked at her sister. "I'd never thought about that."

Alyce bit her lower lip. "Me either. Why would we when The Chocolate Shoppe women are the logical culprits?"

"But we aren't! I came over here today because I was sure you were behind everything that's been going on at our bakery. I'm tired of this battle. I wanted to talk to you and see if we could work something out."

They wore their surprise in identical expressions.

"Why, hello, Jillian!" an overly cheerful voice called out. She turned to see Leslie Phipps, in a bright-yellow dress, grinning at her. "What are you doing here? Listen, try the Crinkle Winks. They are so crunchy and delish! Oh, and be sure to get at least a pound of orange fudge." She patted her tummy with one hand. "I start the potato-and-turnip diet tomorrow, so I'm having one last hurrah with sweets today!" She looked at Alyce. "Hi there. I'm here for Megan's order. She called it in earlier. Two dozen glazed, please."

"It's right here." Alyce reached under the counter and pulled out two pink-and-white striped boxes. "I've already charged her account, and the receipt is taped to the bottom, as usual."

"Goody! Y'all have a nice day. See you later, Jillian."

"That woman gives me hives," Breanna said as the door closed on Leslie.

"Me too," her sister said.

Breanna turned to Jillian. "So do you think there is room in Moss Hollow for two bakeries?"

"I believe it's possible. Don't you?"

Maudie and Wanda Jean entered the bakery and spotted Jillian immediately. They gaped at her in surprise, then looked away, their faces turning red as they hurried to a table.

"Moss Hollow has a rather small population," Alyce said, "but I don't see why we both can't exist peacefully in this town."

"Absolutely," Jillian said.

"But that means no more ugly phone calls or letters."

The iron band in Jillian's stomach twisted. "As I said, I know nothing about those, and if you've received them, no one from The Chocolate Shoppe has done it." She paused and pointed to the wrinkled paper still lying on the counter. "Am I to assume neither of you knows anything about this note we found this morning, or the newspaper article and letter to the editor published in the *Chronicle*?"

Breanna grabbed the note and read it. "Someone sent this to you?"

"It was taped to our front door this morning."

Breanna frowned and hurried away, disappearing down a hallway, but returned a few moments later with a file folder. She took out copies of lined notebook paper on which was written, *Leave town and no one will get hurt.* Another read, *Take your snooty selves and big business back to the city.* A third proclaimed, *If you leave voluntarily, you can leave in one piece.*

These missives were far more serious than anything The Chocolate Shoppe had received. "When did you get these?"

"Last week," Alyce said. "We've gotten others but threw them away."

"We started getting calls before the bakery opened," Breanna said. "Our house was egged once, and someone left something from a barnyard on our front porch. Even worse, someone poured paint all over my new car the night before the grand opening. And don't forget that fire that destroyed our building supplies."

"That's terrible." Jillian was shocked.

"Yes, it is. Not a very nice way to welcome us into the community."

"Then the pranks and harassment stopped," Alyce said. "We thought whoever was doing it realized Confections & Donuts wasn't leaving just because of hooliganism, and they'd given up."

"But three days ago we both got a letter in our mailbox at home, and yesterday a third one was in our mailbox here at the bakery. No address, no stamp. Just folded in thirds in a blank envelope. We kept the notes this time and have started a record of the phone calls."

"Did you go to the sheriff?"

They looked at each other. "Yes, we did, for what little good it'll do us. He kept the originals of these notes, but seemed rather dismissive. We thought the culprit was probably you or your aunts or one of your employees."

"None of us would ever do something so low-down and dirty."

Breanna crossed her arms. "Yet you accuse of us smearing your shop."

"That's because I don't know you ladies, and because a campaign against The Chocolate Shoppe had never happened until you came to town, so it seemed logical to me that you want to shut us down."

"Kindly remember that we don't know you either, Ms. Green."

They all regarded one another for an awkward moment.

"I suppose there is no way we will completely trust each other, is there?" Jillian said.

"Not until that trust is built and proven."

"All right. How about this?" Jillian said. "Let's give each other a second chance. We will stop thinking the worst of you and Confections & Donuts, if you will cease to belittle and jeer at The Chocolate Shoppe."

The twins looked at each other, then nodded. "One condition," Breanna said.

"Which is?" Jillian hoped her competitior was not about to ask that they recommend Confections & Donuts to The Chocolate Shoppe customers.

"That we're allowed to attend the Sweetie Pies meetings and be welcomed rather than resented. We love baking, and we do want to be part of the community here."

"Of course. As long as you agree not to start a competing baking club. The Southern Sweetie Pies mean a lot to Bertie, Cornelia, and Lenora."

They turned away and whispered together, then faced her and said, "All right."

"And I strongly urge you to trust Sheriff Henderson. He may come across as dismissive, but I can assure you he is not. He's not a talker, but he sure is a doer. He takes good care of Moss Hollow, so he'll take good care of you and your bakery."

For the first time since she'd known them, both sisters turned from portrayals of cold businesswomen into real people. A barb of guilt poked her conscience for refusing to take a step toward cooperation earlier. She hoped they were being truthful with her.

"We'll see you Sunday afternoon, then."

They nodded, like a matched set.

When Jillian returned to The Chocolate Shoppe, Rick Drummond sat at one of the tables, sipping coffee and chatting with Bertie and Lenora.

"Here she is at last," Bertie said. "Where have you been all this time?"

"I had an errand to run. Hello, Rick." She met his eyes and remembered the kiss. She felt a little awkward. "I need some coffee. Do you want some more?"

"Sit down. Rick wants to talk to us, and we've been waiting for you."

She settled next to Rick, the only empty chair at the table. "What's up?"

"He says he has the answer to our troubles."

She raised both brows. "Oh?"

"I don't know. We've been waiting on you because he insisted you be here."

"I see." Jillian turned to him. "So tell us, what's the answer to our troubles?"

He leaned forward and peered into each woman's face. Instinctively, they leaned in too.

"The other night at Belle Haven, I told you how much I've come to love Moss Hollow in the short time I've been here. Remember?" They all nodded, looking at him expectantly. "The small-town atmosphere, the personal and family values that seem old-fashioned in today's world are so refreshing to me. I'd hate to see our community go the way of many small towns when big businesses take over. Downtown deterioration. Neighborhoods swept away in the name of progress and money."

"You got that right, honey," Lenora said.

"I don't want it to happen to Moss Hollow."

"Neither do we."

He shifted a bit in his chair. "I've been looking for another investment, and this time I want it to be something that will make a difference for others. So I had a fantastic idea. I talked with my bank, and I can afford it." He paused and smiled at each of them. "Let me take this old building off your hands and restore it."

"*What?*" Bertie's expression was completely mystified. Jillian and Lenora stared at him as if he'd grown a second head.

"Let me buy this place from you and renovate it. When I'm finished, if you still want to have a bakery, I can lease it to you at a fair price."

Time seemed frozen. Then they leaned back in their seats, gawping at him and at one another.

"This is completely unexpected," Jillian said.

"Completely," Bertie echoed. "Why would you want to do such a thing?"

"Didn't you hear him say he wanted to make an investment that would help others?" Lenora said.

"I agree with Bertie." Jillian turned to Rick. "Why would you do this?"

He lost his smile. "Do you think I have something nefarious up my sleeve?" He looked at Bertie. "Do you?"

She frowned and looked uneasy. "That's not what Jillian meant, I'm sure, and certainly not why I'm hesitant. It's just that we are virtually strangers to each other."

"I'm an observer of people, and maybe I flatter myself by thinking I can spot the differences between honorable and dishonorable almost upon a first meeting. Plus, your reputation in this town proves you are well-known and loved. You are highly respected within the community." He paused as if letting his words find their mark. "And I'd be happy to provide you with references as to my own character and background."

"Don't you think this is kind of coming out of the blue?" Lenora asked him.

"I suppose it seems so to you." He gave her a reassuring smile. "However, as I said, I have my resources and contacts, and to be perfectly honest, this is something I've had in mind for a while. All I needed was the right business and the right people." He turned to Bertie. "I can have the money to buy you out by the end of the week."

"What?" Bertie gawked at him.

"What resources and contacts?" Lenora asked.

"Think about it, Bertie. No more worry about competition or bad press. If something spoils or vermin runs through the place during business hours, you won't have to deal with it." He gripped one of her hands and looked almost pleadingly into her eyes. "It would be such a blessing for me to do this for you, especially given the trouble you've been through lately."

"I—We have to talk about this, Rick," she choked out. "Lenora, Jillian, and I. And my sister. I can't just—" She spread the fingers of her free hand.

Disappointment shot across his features, but he nodded. "Of course. I fully understand. But don't wait too long. The fellow who's investing with me has his eye on another project, which has far more appeal to him than a small bakery. So you ladies discuss it and get back me to as soon as you can."

Shortly before Jillian locked the front door for the day, Savannah hurried into the bakery. Her face was flushed and her breath came in quick bursts. The Chocolate Shoppe was empty of all customers, and Bertie had already gone home. Lenora and Jillian remained, taking care of end-of-the-day business.

"Guess who I saw not more than ten minutes ago?" Savannah said.

"Santa Claus?" Lenora offered.

"Not quite. I saw Gordon Brett coming out of Bailey's Farm Supply."

"Buying some new overalls, was he?" Lenora asked. "That boy might clean up right nice if he was ever to shave and wear something spiffy."

"Lenora, please. Did you talk to him, Savannah?"

"No, I was in the car. By the time I turned around to go back to him, he was nowhere in sight."

"I'll tell you something," Lenora said. "He's a right peculiar fellow. Don't believe we've exchanged more than twenty words. When he comes in here, he gets what he wants and out the door he goes with barely a howdy-do."

"I wonder how long he's been back from wherever he went," Savannah said.

"I've driven past his place every evening, and he's not been home."

"That you know of," Lenora said. "He may have been hiding out in the woods all this time."

"Why would he hide out in the woods when he has a perfectly nice house to live in?"

"To hide from the law, of course," Lenora said. "Why else?"

"As far as we know, Gordon has done nothing illegal," Savannah reminded her.

The three of them looked at one another, but none of them had a logical explanation concerning the man or his absence.

"Let's go over to his place after you close," Savannah said to Jillian.

"The last time we tried that, you were pretty lily-livered."

"That was at night, and it was dark. Besides, I was dead tired. So, when you—"

"You ain't goin' anywhere right after work, either one of you. Have you forgotten Bertie wants to get together soon as we eat supper? And she wants you there too, Savannah."

"I had forgotten," Jillian admitted. "We'll go to Gordon's after the meeting."

"Or wait until tomorrow and go in the daylight," Savannah said. "Why are we having another meeting?"

"It's a matter that concerns all of us and The Chocolate Shoppe."

"I'll be there."

16

"Another family meeting." Cornelia sighed. "I hope this doesn't get to be a regular thing."

"Aunt Cornelia." Jillian put a shushing finger to her lips.

"I wasn't at the other family meeting," Lenora said.

"You didn't miss much. And that's all I'm saying." Cornelia folded her arms and pressed her lips together as if she'd never speak again for as long as she lived.

Bertie stood at the head of the table in the dining room and rapped the tabletop with her knuckles. "This meeting will come to order."

"Are we supposed to take notes this time too?" Cornelia piped up.

"You are supposed to *listen*."

"Go ahead, Judge Judy. I'm all ears."

Jillian nudged her great-aunt's foot with her own. Cornelia shifted, raised her chin, and stared at Bertie as if she were on display.

"We need to talk about Rick Drummond's proposal—"

"Proposal?" Cornelia looked at Jillian. "He didn't propose already, did he? At least give the matter some thought before you do anything that drastic."

"Cornelia Montgomery! Be quiet, please." Bertie glowered at her. "This kind of chatter is exactly why I wanted to meet with the contractor alone, and why I suggested Rick talk to us at the bakery instead of here. You can be distracting."

"Well, if that don't beat all, Bertie. I'm distracting?"

"It's a simple fact that you go off on tangents and distract everyone. There are times when it can be an endearing, if rather annoying, trait. But when it comes to business matters, we need to stay focused."

"Fine. Go ahead." Cornelia leaned toward Jillian and whispered, "I know how to keep my mouth shut."

Bertie cleared her throat. "For Cornelia and Savannah who weren't present this morning, I'll go over what Rick presented to us. Jillian and Lenora, please make sure I have my information correct."

She relayed the details of Rick's offer, adding that while they didn't know him well, he had certainly taken an interest in Moss Hollow. He seemed to want to help the town in general and The Chocolate Shoppe in particular.

"Also, he will furnish us with references. I think he's to be commended for his civic spirit," she concluded.

"References for what?" Cornelia asked.

"I assume character references as to his honesty and integrity. Business references as to his work ethics and skills. Financial references as to his ability to do what he says he will do. But before we talk about that, let's revisit the pros and cons of selling the bakery."

"What do we know about his finances?" Cornelia looked around. "For all we know he might be as rich as Midas or poorer than Job's turkey."

Jillian cleared her throat. "Before we go any further with this, I think you should know something I learned this morning while I was out."

"Does it have anything to do with the subject at hand?" Bertie asked.

"I believe so."

"All right. Then go ahead."

"I went to Confections & Donuts this morning."

"You did what?" Cornelia asked. "Why Jillian Green, who said you should do that?"

"Cornelia," Savannah said, "why don't we let Jillian tell us why she was there and what she learned?"

"I'll try to make this short and sweet. I believe we may have been making some erroneous assumptions—"

"Don't tell me you're taking their side against me!" Bertie said.

She turned to her grandmother. "Of course not. I went over there to find out what they knew about the article and letter in the newspaper or the note on the door or any other underhanded nonsense that has been going on."

"Note on the door?" Savannah asked. "What note?"

"Something we found on the door of The Chocolate Shoppe earlier today," Jillian explained.

"And did they fess up?" Lenora's folded arms and thrust-out chin clearly proved her suspicion.

"They said they knew nothing about anything that had—"

"There you go." Bertie flapped a dismissive hand. "You wasted your time trying to get them to do the right thing."

Jillian blew out a breath of exasperation. "I wish you'd just let me tell you what I found out."

"Go ahead. Tell." Bertie averted her eyes and stared at a point on the wall. The disgust on her face was thick enough to roll into a crust and bake.

"They've been on the receiving end of worse pranks than we have." She finally had the undivided attention of all four of them. "Alyce and Breanna have received phone calls and letters, many of them containing threats of violence. Breanna has had her car vandalized, and they think someone has been in their house. Neither woman feels safe in Moss Hollow."

Complete silence fell for several seconds.

"Are you sure they weren't just pulling your leg, trying to get sympathy?" Lenora asked. "Jillian, you're a strong woman, but sometimes your heart is too soft."

"Be that as it may, I saw the letters. Three of them, handwritten on notebook paper, and they were very nasty."

"How do you know they didn't write those themselves?" Cornelia said.

"I suppose it's possible that they did, but there's no good reason to do something so foolish. I'm positive they didn't pour paint on a brand-new luxury car, and no one would egg her own house. And anyway, I also saw how frightened they are. You know that look Bertie has had in her eyes lately? The one that worries us all? Breanna and Alyce have that same fear in their eyes."

"Is it possible that someone else is likely trying to ruin both bakeries?" Savannah asked.

Jillian nodded. "Maybe. It's something I've been wondering."

Lenora frowned. "But who?"

"Maybe it's someone who wants to open their own," Bertie said. "Three bakeries in our little town would be too many."

"There's more," Jillian said. "The Sherman sisters want to join the Sweetie Pies, and I told them they could."

Bertie and Cornelia gasped, Savannah's eyebrows went up, and Lenora yelped.

"They want to be a part of the community, and I think we should give them the opportunity." When no one said anything, she added, "If we can all get along with one another, this ugly competition between Confections & Donuts and The Chocolate Shoppe can become a healthier business move. For all of us."

Again the women sat in silence, each staring at some point in her own vision as Jillian's words settled.

"Let's consider this latest news as we continue," Bertie said. She pulled a sheet of yellow paper from the pocket of her slacks and unfolded it. "I have a pros and cons list, so let's go down it point by point."

For the next two hours, the women discussed every aspect of selling The Chocolate Shoppe, weighing every alternative idea they could concoct. Cornelia's remarks and observations were also plain and concise, proving she still possessed sharp wits and knew how to use them.

By the end of the evening, the decision had been made, and the women were exhausted.

"Shall I call Rick and tell him?" Bertie asked before she headed to her bedroom.

Jillian shook her head. "No, it's late. Tomorrow is soon enough."

The next morning, Jillian drove to Gordon Brett's. If the family meeting hadn't taken the whole of yesterday evening, she would have gone then. She pulled up the long drive and parked, looking around for any sign of her neighbor. She didn't have to look hard or wait long. Gordon came around from the back of the house and strode toward her.

"Good morning, Jillian," he called cheerfully as she got out of the car.

"Hi, Gordon." She studied his face as he got closer. No telltale sign of insanity, duplicity, threat, or anger lay in his features. "We've been worried about you."

His smile faded some. "You have? Why?"

"Because you've been gone for quite awhile."

He frowned. "You've been keeping tabs on me?"

"Not at all. That is, no more than we would keep tabs on any friend or neighbor who suddenly seemed to disappear. I've stopped by your house almost every day, looking for you."

His eyes narrowed.

Maybe I shouldn't have said it quite that way.

"Why?"

This is Gordon. I'm not afraid of Gordon.

But how could she explain why she'd been to his house so often that week unless she confronted him about his presence on the front lawn?

Get a grip. You were prepared to meet him face-to-face in the woods that night.

She drew in a deep breath. "Savannah and I saw you outside Belle Haven one night."

He looked surprised. "Why didn't you say anything?"

She stared at him in surprise. "Because you seemed to be hiding, and then you disappeared."

He took off his straw hat and scratched his head, frowning. "Why would you think that?"

"Because you were lurking behind the trees, and then you slipped away. Besides, I did call out to you, several times."

He settled the hat back onto his head and met her eyes straight on.

"Get this straight. I wasn't hiding, lurking, or slipping away. I had walked over to Belle Haven along the road because I wanted to tell you ladies that I was going to Atlanta for a couple weeks. But I overheard you and Savannah talking about how worried and upset Miss Bertie was with that new bakery, and I didn't want to intrude."

"But we saw you go into the woods and back toward your house. When we got there, you weren't home."

"No, I walked on into town and caught the bus."

She trawled through her memory of that night. "Oh, yeah, now I remember—we weren't sure we actually saw you in the woods. It was breezy that night, and there was a lot of movement in the shadows from tree limbs and bushes."

His expression was frozen and unreadable. "You went to my house to see why I was sneaking around your place?"

Her face grew hot, but she refused to drop her gaze. "Yes. It was a little unsettling to see you out front, then not be able to find you. It was night. We've had a lot going on lately, and I guess my mind was ready to take off on a tangent."

His jaw muscles relaxed and the narrowness left his eyelids. "I understand that. Imagination can be a powerful tool. If you're tired or worried, your mind will concoct some incredible scenarios for you to think about."

"Yes, it does."

An awkward silence lay between them. Jillian was thinking about the fire, and no doubt his thoughts followed the same line. She recalled Alyce saying that the calls and notes to Confections & Donuts had ceased for a while but had started again.

"How long have you been back, Gordon?"

"I got back yesterday." He began walking along pathways through the garden beds, pausing to examine a leaf or uproot a weed. Jillian trailed behind, and he spoke to her over his shoulder. "I rigged up a timer to keep the plants watered. They've grown so much. I've got a lot of work to catch up on."

"It doesn't take long for plants to grow this time of year. You're going to be busy."

"I always am." He glanced at her. "You were so anxious to find me, and now that you have, aren't you the least bit interested where I've been and what I was doing?"

Something in his voice and the expression on his face told her he knew she suspected him of dark deeds. She was more than a little curious about his recent activities, but felt uneasy expressing it.

"I'll admit that I'm interested."

"Okay, since you twisted my arm." He gave her a wry grin. "I went to some garden shows and conventions in Atlanta and surrounding areas. I attended gardening seminars and purchased a variety of heirloom seeds. But my main purpose was to go to the capitol building and talk to our state representative about protecting Moss Hollow from the encroachment of corporate interests."

She gave herself a moment to absorb his words. Gardens, plants, seeds. Of course that would be something Gordon would do. As for the other, given his gentle nature, seeking a legal solution to what he perceived as a threat made far more sense than him indulging in criminal mischief and threats of violence.

"And what did you find out?"

He scowled and made an impatient gesture. "Nothing. There is nothing anyone can do because we live in a country of free enterprise. So, if someone has enough money, he can do what he wants, where he wants, when he wants."

"Well, only up to a point."

"Yeah, and that point seems mighty dim most of the time." He kicked a clod of dirt and nudged out a shallow-rooted weed with the toe of his boot. "I'm not giving up on this, but right now, my attention has to be focused on these gardens. There's a lot of folks who will benefit from the harvest of these plants, but only if I keep working. No more trips to Atlanta for a while."

He bent to examine a young tomato plant and began quietly humming an old hymn. Jillian waited for him to say more, but he seemed to have forgotten she was there, so she quietly left him to his garden.

As she drove to the bakery, she mulled over their conversation. Apparently he hadn't set the fire or vandalized the Sherman twins' property. He hadn't written letters to them or to the editor of the newspaper. He certainly hadn't been around to turn rats loose in The Chocolate Shoppe.

So who did?

17

The bakery was moderately busy when Jillian got there, and she heard the quiet sound of customers chatting with one another. She was tying her apron when Rick walked in carrying a leather briefcase. She thought he'd looked great before in casual shirts and jeans, but he looked even better in dark-gray slacks, a long-sleeved white shirt, and a silvery-gray tie.

And here I am in my bakery garb and apron, with my hair slicked back like a lunch lady. She reminded herself it didn't matter what she looked like. Rick was not on her radar as anything resembling a romantic interest. If she'd wanted that with him, she could have had it. She just hoped if Hunter walked in, she'd have time to brush her hair and pinch some color into her cheeks.

"Good morning." He greeted them with a smile. His eyes shone, and his expression was full of hope.

Bertie looked at Lenora and Jillian, drew in a deep breath, and smoothed her apron.

"Good morning, Rick. Lenora has offered us the use of her apartment for a private meeting this morning."

He raised one eyebrow as though this surprised him, but nodded. "All right."

"Jillian, you come with us. Lenora, you and Maggie mind the shop. We'll be back."

Bertie led the way up to Lenora's small, immaculate apartment.

"Have a seat, Rick." She indicated the settee. Jillian chose the cozy armchair. Bertie perched on the edge of her seat and turned to Rick. "After you left us last night, we had a lengthy family discussion."

"There were a lot of points to consider, I'm sure," Rick said. "There always are when we face major life changes."

"Yes, indeed. And life changes are more daunting the older we get."

"Aw, now, Bertie. You aren't getting older. You are ripening into a stage of beauty and wisdom."

She narrowed her eyes. "Don't say things like that. It makes you sound insincere, especially when you say it to someone my age."

He winced. "I meant no offense."

"And none was taken. I'm just offering you some of my ripened wisdom. Most people can spot flattery, and it will turn them right off. But I like you." She patted his hand and gave his fingers a squeeze. "So you don't need to try to win me over."

His face lit up. "Wonderful! I have all the paperwork." He settled the briefcase in his lap and opened it. "Now, first is the—"

"I'm sorry to interrupt you, Rick," Bertie said, "but there's no reason for me to waste your time letting you tell me about all that."

His eyes moved quickly from Bertie to Jillian and back to Bertie.

"We're not selling The Chocolate Shoppe."

"No?" He looked wounded. "Is my offer not generous enough? Remember I said you could lease it . . . no?"

Bertie was shaking her head emphatically.

"No. We went over our list, item by item: what needs to be done—we want to build on to the back, giving us a bigger kitchen and storage room and a large dining area—our savings, our ability to get the work done, and the time it will take. It will drain the money we had put aside to remodel the kitchen at Belle Haven, but we can manage it, if we're thrifty and smart."

"But don't you want to retire, Bertie? Don't you want to sleep late, pad around in your slippers and pajamas until noon, and enjoy your golden years in rest and relaxation? It would be so good for you."

Bertie gawked at him as if he'd lost his mind.

"What an absurd notion. Do I get tired? Yes. Would I like to sleep late some mornings? Yes. But does that mean I'm going to give up my life and livelihood just to become self-indulgent? I might be nearly eighty, but I'm not old."

He stared at her for several moments then turned to Jillian. "What do you have to say about this, Jillian? Don't you think your grandmother deserves to live a life of ease after so many years of hard work?"

She looked at Bertie and felt such a stir of warmth, love, and understanding that her throat closed and tears stung her eyes.

"I stand with her, whatever her decision. Bertie deserves the life she wants, not the life others think she should have."

A long silence followed and he kept looking at them as if expecting one or the other to change her mind. Finally, he closed the briefcase and laid both palms on it.

"Are you sure? This is a great deal, and I'd love to help you. You've become very dear to me in a very short time."

"Bless your heart," Bertie said, "but our minds are made up. We aren't selling this bakery to anyone. But if we were to do so, it would be to you."

His face softened, and he leaned over for the kiss she planted on his cheek. "That means more than the sale of a bakery," he said. "Thank you."

He got to his feet, and offered them a smile full of sweet sadness. "Turned down by two lovely women."

"I'm sure there are plenty of other opportunities for you in Moss Hollow," Bertie said.

"Yes. I have my eye on a couple of other ventures. Everything works out as it should." He turned to Jillian. "I wish some things had worked out differently, though."

Her face burned, but she said, "Thanks for the offer, Rick. Both of them."

He nodded. "I'll see myself out the back. 'Bye, now."

Bertie grabbed Jillian's arm before she could reach the door. "What did you mean, 'both of them'?"

"Bertie," she sighed, "right now, I'd rather not talk about it."

Jillian went to bed earlier than usual that night. She and Hunter had a date to attend a singing at Apple Grove Church, a little country church a few miles out of town. With all the stress that had been happening over the last couple of weeks, her sleep had been unusually fitful and often cut short. The last thing she wanted when Hunter came to pick her up the next evening was to look worn out.

She turned off her lamp, turned on a CD of relaxation music, and placed cool, damp tea bags on her closed eyes. The windows in her bedroom were open and a soft breeze billowed in. She sighed, and felt herself slip into soft darkness.

Some time later, the smell of smoke woke her up. She sat up, sniffing, tense, wondering about the source.

Are the woods on fire?

She swung her legs off the bed and hurried to the window. She cupped her hands around her eyes and peered outside, seeking flames, seeing nothing. Turning from the window, she faced her open bedroom door, then rushed toward it. The scent of smoke was stronger and she ran toward the staircase. An unusual glow flickered downstairs. Her heart stopped, then leaped against her ribs.

"Fire!" she screamed. "Bertie, Aunt Cornelia!"

She ran to Cornelia's bedroom and flung open the door, shouting, "Fire! Get up and get outside. Fire!"

Cornelia stirred and sat up.

"Hurry! Get outside as fast as you can."

She grabbed the woman's arm and pulled her along, rushing down the stairs. The burning smell was stronger, and the darkened rooms were dim with smoke.

"Outside, now!"

She pushed her toward the door and ran to Bertie's room, screaming her name.

"Bertie!" She threw open the door and shook her grandmother awake. "Get up. There's a fire in the house. Get up!"

"Wha—?"

Jillian yanked off the covers and hauled her out of the bed. She grabbed the robe and a blanket and hustled her out.

"Where is it?" Bertie stumbled, stopped, stared. "The kitchen!"

Jillian dropped the blanket and robe, nearly wrestling with Bertie to keep her from running to the burning room.

"You have to leave. Get out!" She shoved the woman onto the veranda where Cornelia stood, big-eyed and shaking. "Get away from the house, both of you. Go out to the yard."

Clinging to each other, the twins scurried down the steps. Jillian dashed back into the house, grabbed Possum, the cordless phone, the blanket, and Bertie's robe.

"Call 911," she ordered, thrusting Possum into Cornelia's hands and the rest into Bertie's.

"Where are you going?" Bertie yelled as Jillian turned back toward Belle Haven.

"The kitchen is pretty well destroyed, but I'm going to get the fire extinguisher and hold off the flames until the fire department can get here."

The Chocolate Shoppe was closed for the day, and they were sitting in Belle Haven's library with the doors closed, away from the damp stench and sight of the ruined kitchen. Members of the Southern Sweetie Pies, neighbors, and friends from church had descended on the mansion, bearing everything from pots of seasoned greens and tuna sandwiches to pot holders, a set of glasses, and a stack of paper plates.

Maudie and Wanda Jean had brought a couple of gallon jars of sweet tea, disposable tumblers, a cooler, and bag of ice. They stood on the doorstep, looking uncomfortable.

"Are we welcome here?" Maudie asked.

An unexpected rush of affection for the two women stirred in Jillian. Somehow, everything dimmed in significance after the events of the last several hours.

"Of course you are. Please come in." Within moments, it was as if the rift in the friendship had never happened. She knew it would have to be addressed and straightened out, but right then, it was enough to have friends back in the circle of fellowship.

"Don't you have a smoke alarm?" Wanda Jean asked a bit later. "I'm sure I saw one in your kitchen once upon a time."

"Of course we did," Jillian said, patting her grandmother's hand. "According to the investigator, the battery had been removed."

"I declare!"

"So it was arson?" Maudie asked.

"Suspicious is what they called it." Jillian said.

"That usually means arson." Wanda Jean passed around a knowing look. "I've seen plenty of true crime on television."

Jillian hated repeating the words once again, but others wanted to know what they'd been through. "Not only had the smoke alarms been tampered with, but an accelerant was used."

"That means someone was in the house besides y'all," Maudie said.

"That seems to be the indication," Cornelia said.

"Someone broke in," Wanda Jean said breathlessly, as if no one else had thought of it.

"Of course someone did. And what's more, the insurance company probably won't pay for the kitchen because of it." Cornelia sat stiffly, glaring at nothing.

"You know that's not true, Aunt Cornelia, unless one of us set the fire. Which we did *not*." Jillian gave her hand a gentle squeeze. "Try not to imagine such wild notions, okay?"

Cornelia sniffled and nodded.

Bertie, who'd been mostly silent for the last several hours, spoke up. Her voice was tremulous as she said, "At least it didn't spread beyond the kitchen. We can be grateful for that."

"Mercy me, yes." Wanda Jean nodded. "We're so glad y'all are safe and Belle Haven is still standing. But who would've done such a thing? What possible purpose could be served by destroying your kitchen?"

"That's a good question for which I have no answer. It's a mercy that none of us were hurt. Jillian was quick-thinking to get us out when she did."

They sat silently for a time, each lost in their own thoughts.

Lenora broke the silence. "We'll do everything we can to help, won't we, folks?"

"Yes, indeed," Maudie said. And the others voiced their willingness.

Hunter Grayson, dressed in a black suit befitting a funeral director, stopped by to drop off a brand-new coffeemaker, a set of white cups, and a three-pound container of ground coffee. He talked with them as he would with any grieving family, in a soft voice filled with comfort and empathy. With a pure-white handkerchief, he blotted away Bertie's and Cornelia's tears, and allowed them to cling to his hands until they wanted to let go.

Watching them and knowing these three important people in her life genuinely cared for one another, Jillian relished the warmth stirring in her heart.

"Before I go, I have something I'm sure you'll appreciate." He removed a magazine from the shopping bag he'd brought in. "I picked up the newest issue of *Southern Roadways*, and guess what?" He opened to a page and handed it Bertie. "Read that."

She read silently, and her face diffused first with surprise, then joy.

"What's it say, what's it say?" Cornelia squinted over her sister's shoulder.

"Read it aloud, Bertie," Jillian said.

Bertie sat up straight and cleared her throat as if about to read before a school assembly.

"'It was our delight to discover Moss Hollow's sweetest treasure, The Chocolate Shoppe Bakery. Tucked in and comfortable on the downtown square, this warm and welcoming little bakery offers the best pastries we found on our tour. Plump doughnuts melt in the mouth. Éclairs with creamy fillings tease the taste buds with just a hint of almond. Brownies with thick fudge frosting transport the happy diner to childhood. The large franchise that recently opened its doors in Moss Hollow can't hold a candle to The Chocolate Shoppe. We give it five candy kisses.'" She looked up, eyes sparkling. "The candy kisses are the rating symbols, and it seems five in the highest."

"That's wonderful, Bertie!" Jillian kissed her cheek, while everyone else agreed.

"I suppose that's what those four women were up to in Stewie Franks's corner that day. Critiquing our food."

"I take back all the nasty things I was thinking about them," Lenora said.

"I'm sure that's very generous." Jillian giggled.

"Don't deny it, girl." Lenora shook a finger at her. "You were thinking the same thing. All of us were."

"I, for one, am glad someone wrote up an expression of what we all know," Hunter said. "Watch your sales go up even more during tourist season. I doubt those four walls will be able to contain everyone."

"We may not have a choice about expansion now," Bertie said, grinning.

After much laughter and a round of encouraging applause, Hunter stood. "I have to get back to work now, but if you need anything at all, please don't hesitate to call me." He looked at Jillian. "You'll see to it that they get in touch if they need anything?"

"Of course. Thank you, Hunter."

He kissed both wrinkled faces, then turned to Jillian. "Walk me to the door?"

She nodded. He wanted to look at the damaged kitchen, and they crossed through the living room to it.

"Wow. It's completely destroyed."

"Completely."

"I am so sorry this happened, Jillian." He slipped one arm around her shoulders and held her close to his side.

"Even in the best of times, a fire destroying part of our home would be horrible. But for it to happen while the business is in peril—it's just too much." She shook her head and fought the sting of tears. She refused to show any weakness or fear around her grandmother and great-aunt, but here, with this wonderful, caring man so close, she could feel herself uncoil from all the stress.

"You know I'll help in any way I can. The cleanup, the rebuild, whatever."

"That means the world to us—and to me. Thank you."

At the front door he started to step outside, but paused and looked down at her. "I assume our date for the singing tonight is postponed."

"It is. They need me."

"That's okay. There will be other times."

"Yes, for sure."

"See you later." He gave her a smile that made her heart skip a beat and then gently kissed her. She stood in the doorway until he had driven out of sight.

Other members of the Southern Sweetie Pies showed up throughout the day bearing gifts of food or wares, and looking for ways to help.

"I'm so glad we've been putting a little money aside from time to time for a long while." Cornelia looked considerably brighter than her sister.

Bertie heaved an enormous sigh. "That money was going to go to expanding the bakery."

"I think the kitchen here at Belle Haven is a priority, Bertie," Jillian said.

"But what about the bakery?"

"Don't you worry about that," Annalise said. "We'll make sure you stay in business, even if we all have to get fatter than a passel of pigs."

Everyone laughed and agreed enthusiastically.

Maudie and Wanda Jean lingered until everyone else left. They fidgeted and looked at each other, then shifted their weight in their chairs. Maudie cleared her throat.

"Um, Bertie?"

"Yes?"

She cleared her throat again. "Uh, Bertie, we—that is, Wanda Jean and I—want to ask your forgiveness. You are one of our dearest friends, and we never meant to hurt you."

Cornelia opened her mouth to speak, but Jillian caught her hand and signaled her to let Bertie reply.

"Yes, you did." Bertie held her gaze.

"But we did some good. We spied on the competition for you,

so if you need to know anything . . ." Wanda Jean's voice trailed off.

"My sister is above spying," Cornelia said sharply. "What you did was get miffed at Jillian and flounce off. I know, because she told me all about it, and my great-niece does not lie."

"But we didn't write that letter!"

"I know that now, and I'm really sorry I hurt your feelings," Jillian said. "It's just that everything has felt so off-balance lately. We've all been looking to blame someone else, it seems. I hope you both forgive me."

A brief and uncomfortable silence fell, then Maudie said, "I forgive you."

"And so do I," Wanda Jean added.

Maudie looked at Bertie. "Jillian accused us of something we'd never do, but we never should have taken that out on you, Bertie. We've missed The Chocolate Shoppe, and all of you. And if you want the honest truth—"

"Always," Bertie said.

Maudie nodded. "I don't know why Confections & Donuts is so popular. Their products are unremarkable. Nothing is as wonderful as they claim."

"And the service is nothing to write home about," Wanda Jean added. "The staff aren't allowed to talk with customers or each other, unless it's related to an order."

"I noticed that the other day," Jillia said. "It seemed like a very unfriendly place."

"I wonder if that's standard rules for Confections & Donuts, or if that's just the Shermans' idea of good business." Maudie curled her lip. "Those two have a lot to learn if they plan to stay in Moss Hollow."

"Wouldn't surprise me a bit if they aren't the ones responsible for your ruined kitchen," Wanda Jean said.

"Really?" Cornelia turned to her. "What makes you think that?"

"Mostly because I can't think of anyone else who would. Can you?"

"No." Cornelia stiffened. "Say, do you remember a few years ago when Rube Faulk broke into folks' houses and stole every bit of food in the refrigerator? He did that for who knows how long until Ike Puckett caught him one night."

"What in the name of time does that have to do with this situation?" Bertie said. "Besides, he's locked up for possession of stolen property."

"Rube got out of the clink back in January. He might be sneaking into kitchens again."

"What a notion."

"Who do you think did it, then?" Cornelia demanded.

Jillian did not want to hear more bickering, and she refused to give Maudie and Wanda Jean fuel for rumors. "We'll just have to wait and see what the investigation turns up."

"Then there's Gordon Brett," Wanda Jean said. "He's a weird one, and he lives nearby. I bet he did it."

"No more speculations right now," Jillian said. "What we need to focus on is making sure we have what we need until that kitchen is back in working order."

"I agree," Savannah said. "And I'll be happy to discuss it further, but I have an errand to run first."

She had been gone less than five minutes when the doorbell rang. Jillian opened the door to find Rick Drummond on the other side of the threshold, several shopping bags in his arms, his face serious, and his eyes full of concern. A delivery truck was backing into the *porte cochere*.

"I heard about the fire out here. I brought you some groceries." He tipped his head toward the truck. "I also brought you a refrigerator to keep them in. I noticed there's an outlet in the carport. We can plug it in there for now if that works for you. Or we can move it into the house somewhere, if you'd rather."

Her mouth dropped open. "My goodness, Rick. Thank you so much! Please come inside. You can set the bags down right there, and—my goodness, what a kind gesture. Come into the library."

This is why he drives an old beater. He spends his money helping others rather than on spending it on himself.

She walked with him into the library, where voices died as they entered. Every female eye gave him an appreciative once-over, but he seemed oblivious.

"I was so very sorry to hear the news," he said.

"Thank you," Bertie said. "It's terrible, but with the support from our friends, I know we'll be all right."

"Rick brought us some groceries. And a fridge to put them in," Jillian said.

"A what?" Bertie said. "Rick, you didn't!"

"I did. It's being set up in the carport right now, but you can move it into the kitchen when you're ready." He went to the twins and hunkered down between them. "Is there anything else I can do? Is there anything you need?"

"My word!" Cornelia stared at him. "Why would you do such a thing?"

"Now why do you think, ma'am? I did it because you need it. I did it because you are fine, generous women, and you deserve good things. I did it because it was the right thing to do."

"Rick, honey," Bertie said, taking one of his hands, "we can't accept—"

"Of course you can, and I insist that you do. If you choose to get rid of it later, there are some fine charities in the area and plenty of needy folks. But I refuse to take it back."

The twins stared at him in silence, their eyes swimming. Jillian blinked back her own tears.

"Thank you," she said. "We gladly accept your generous offer."

Bertie and Cornelia turned their gazes to her for just a moment, then nodded and gave Rick big smiles.

"Thank you," they said in unison.

"And all we brought was a cooler and some ice," Wanda Jean said.

"Which is greatly appreciated," Jillian assured her. "Along with all the other contributions folks have been making today."

"That's the truth," Bertie said. "Everyone has been so good and kind." Tears continued to well in her eyes. She wiped them with the back of her hand and got to her feet. "Let's go take a look at that fridge."

Maudie and Wanda Jean left soon after everyone had oohed and ahhed over the large stainless steel refrigerator with all the racks, drawers, and shelf space anyone could ask for. Maudie took a photo with her phone, declaring Hugh was going to buy them one just like it or she'd stop cooking.

"I can't wait for Savannah to get back from her errand so she can get a gander at this," Cornelia said, peeking one more time inside the sleek appliance before going back into the house.

Lenora left soon after they did, hugging everyone who remained. "Work tomorrow?"

"Yep. Business as usual," Bertie assured her. "We can't afford to leave the bakery shut down more than one day."

"See you bright and early, then."

Back in the library Rick lingered, sipping the sweet tea Wanda Jean and Maudie had brought.

Soon Savannah returned, nodding to Rick and Jillian before walking straight to Bertie.

"Here are the claim papers you need to fill out for the insurance company." She placed the manila envelope on the antique cherry desk. "They much prefer you do this online, though."

Cornelia waved one hand. "We're not putting our private information out there for the whole world to see and steal our identity. That's all the online world is good for. Nearly as bad as those scammer phone calls trying to pry out every bit of information from a person."

"It's okay, Cornelia." Savannah gave her a reassuring smile. "That's why I have the paper forms for you."

"You're a good one," Bertie said. She looked around. "When you get right down to it, fire or not, we are so blessed. We still have our home, we have each other, we have friends both old and new, and we still have the business."

Rick was silent and serious, looking out the window, appearing to be lost in thought.

"Rick? Do you have something on your mind?" Cornelia said.

"Pardon?" He turned. "Oh, do I have something on my mind? Yes, ma'am. Actually I do." He crossed the room and settled on the edge of one of the armchairs. Resting his elbows on his knees, he leaned forward. "Coming back inside a bit ago, I looked at that kitchen and thanked God the fire went no farther."

"Yes, we are all so very thankful for that," Savannah said, and the others agreed.

"I wish I could help rebuild it for you."

"Bless your heart," Bertie said. "We've saved for a few years just for a kitchen remodel. Our insurance should pay for the damage, even if it was arson. If not, we'll use the money for its original purpose instead of expanding the bakery."

He moved a little nearer the edge of his seat. "That's exactly what I was thinking about. Bertie, my offer is still on the table to buy the bakery, renovate it, then lease it to you."

"*No.*"

Rick jerked back and frowned.

Bertie put her fingers to her mouth and looked apologetic. "That came out a little snappier than I intended. It's just that I feel everything is trying to slip from my fingers."

"I understand," he said softly.

"I do appreciate your generous offer, though, and I know it comes from the heart."

"Yes, it does." He nodded. "It sure does. You ladies know how much you've come to mean to me in such a short time."

"We know, and we feel the same about you. But the fact is the bakery is my legacy and will be Jillian's, and I'm not selling it."

He sat unmoving for a few moments, as if waiting for her to change her mind. Then he relaxed, smiled warmly, and nodded again.

"I understand, and I commend you for being strong in your resolve to care for your granddaughter. Family comes first, always."

They chatted a while longer, then he took his leave, reminding them to call him if they needed anything.

"What a lovely young man." Cornelia sighed. "Savannah, you should go after him."

"I don't chase after strangers." She laughed. "Besides, James and I are in a good place right now."

"Oh really?" Jillian teased. Savannah's face pinked. "I'm happy for you, Savannah."

"You're the one who goes chasing boys, sister," Bertie reminded Cornelia. "You chased poor Toby Butler until he moved off to North Carolina."

Cornelia frowned. "I did?" Her face cleared. "That was in the third grade, for goodness' sake."

"Still. There are times when I think you could slip right back into that boy-crazy phase."

Lenora returned later in the afternoon, an overnight bag in her hand.

"I don't think I can rest for worrying about those two women," she announced when Jillian opened the door. "It's worse than worrying about rats in the apartment. May I stay with you tonight?"

"You are more than welcome to stay here anytime."

She stepped inside, shaking her head. "I guess there's not much I can do if the place was to catch fire again, but I can help to keep an eye on things, in case someone comes sneaking around with matches. I'll make sure we're all safe and sound." She patted her overnight case and winked.

"What? You plan to clunk an intruder over the head with that thing?"

Bertie came into the foyer. "I heard that. Lenora, did you borrow Hattie Florence's old revolver?"

Jillian groaned. "You didn't bring a gun here, did you, Lenora?"

Lenora gave her a beatific smile and strolled into the living room. She pointed at the sofa. "I'll sleep right there. Nobody'll get past me—I sleep with one eye open."

"You keep that pistol in that case under your underwear and socks, you hear me?" Bertie said. "Don't you be shooting at anyone."

"If nobody comes in, then nobody gets hurt." She set her jaw, and it was clear no power on earth would change her mind.

19

Cornelia and Bertie went to bed at sundown that evening. Lenora took them warm milk and cinnamon toast. When Jillian checked on each of them a bit later, neither moved in her bed.

"Dead to the world, both of them," she told Savannah and Lenora.

"I just hope all this stress doesn't make either of them sick," Lenora said.

"Me too."

"We'll just make sure to take care of them," Savannah added.

"Absolutely." Jillian flopped down on the sofa and tucked her legs beneath her. She was tired to the bone but too keyed up to rest.

"Don't let either of them hear you say that *you're* going to take care of *them*." Lenora had brought a ball of bright-orange yarn with her and was knitting rapidly. "You two had better hope and pray you're as spry as they are when you're their age."

"I pray for that every day."

They were in the sitting room, Jillian and Lenora on the sofa, an empty pizza box on the coffee table in front of them. Dry groceries had been stored in the library, and perishables were safely tucked away in the new refrigerator humming quietly in the porte cochere. The windows of Belle Haven had been open all day with fans running to flush the damp, smoky smell out of the house.

Savannah sat on the floor near one end of the coffee table, sifting through papers she'd found in a charred metal box.

"What's that?" Jillian asked.

"Something that was in the kitchen. It was half-buried in an ashy pile near the door where that cupboard used to be. I thought it might have something useful inside."

"Bertie and Cornelia have always liked to store keepsakes in old enamel boxes," Lenora said, peering briefly over the top of her reading glasses at the blackened container. "That's probably one of them."

"It is. Some old letters, some photos. I was hoping to find money or a bond, something like that."

Jillian scooched to the edge of the sofa and dipped her hand into the trove. She brought out a postcard from St. Paul, Minnesota, with a brief note about snowy roads. It had been signed, *Your friend, M.* There was also a shopping list in Bertie's handwriting, a dried-up ballpoint pen, a lace-trimmed handkerchief, and one of Jillian's school photos.

She grimaced at it. "*Blech.* Too much big hair. What else is in there?" She laid the stuff aside and reached for more.

"Here's a clipping." Savannah unfolded the yellowed newspaper and read a bit of it. "It was about the time the plumbing broke somewhere at the back of The Chocolate Shoppe."

Jillian laughed. "That made news? The *Chronicle* must have been as hard up for stories back then as it is now."

"I remember that." Lenora looked up from her knitting. "What a mess out there in the back. Those pipes were as old as Methuselah and rusty. Best I recall, we had to close down a few days, and so did businesses nearby."

Savannah finished the short article and handed it to Jillian, who read it with interest.

"Hey, listen to this: 'We look forward to being back to normal soon,' said Bertie Harper, owner of The Chocolate Shoppe." She put the piece aside, laughing. "I'm surprised a breaking news story like that didn't make headlines across the state, or even the nation."

Savannah giggled.

"Tsk, tsk. Is that any way to talk?" Lenora peered over the tops of her glasses again, trying and failing to look stern.

"Probably not. What else is in that box, Savannah?"

"Just these photos." She handed over three pictures. "A tarnished silver chain, and a dried rose with a ribbon on it."

Jillian glanced at the chain and the flower, then turned her attention to the photographs. The first one was a shot of a younger Bertie and Cornelia. They stood side by side outside the Moss Hollow Community Church, Bibles clasped to their chests, big smiles on their faces. She flipped it over and read aloud, "'B&C last Easter.'" The next photo was a shot of the chamber of commerce building in its early stages of being built. Looking at it reminded her of Megan Farley. She preferred not to think of the woman and put the snapshot aside.

The last picture showed two young men in workman's coveralls standing next to each other. A blond man was leaning on a shovel, and a dark-haired man with wire-frame glasses stood with his hands on his hips as if taking a rest. Both of them were grinning at the camera. On the back was written *Earl Drumm (R) and Chuck Stanifer (L)*. Something about the dark-haired man—Earl, according to the back of the photo—caught her attention.

"Do either of you know an Earl Drumm or Chuck Stanifer?"

"Don't sound familiar to me," Lenora said.

Savannah looked up from trying to work knots out of the silver chain. "I've never heard of them."

"Me either, but look at that guy on the right. Seems like I've seen him, but the names aren't familiar."

Savannah took the photo and studied it. She jerked upright and held it closer, then turned on the lamp next to the sofa and held it under the light.

"Jillian, look again."

She held the photo under the light as Savannah had and squinted hard at it. Recognition nearly knocked her over.

"Is it . . .?"

"I'm sure it is. He's dyed his hair."

"And shaved his mustache."

"And got rid of his glasses."

"Who?" Lenora said.

"It's him," Savannah said. "I'm almost positive."

"But why? When?"

They stared at each other in a dumbfounded silence

Lenora put down her knitting and held out one hand. "Let me see what has you so bumfuzzled."

Jillian passed the photo to her. "You recognize him?"

She squinted at it. "Which one?"

"The guy with the mustache."

She studied the image, then finally shook her head. "I don't know him. He looks a little familiar maybe, but not much. Why? Who do you think he is?"

"Before I go making assumptions and putting ideas into your head, I need to check something first." She got out her phone and typed in the name *Earl Drumm*. Savannah was already typing in her phone.

"Well, if the both of you are gonna be on your phones instead of talking to me," Lenora said with a sniff, "I'm gonna work on these slippers."

The only sound for the next few moments was the sound of tapping and beeping. Then Savannah gasped. A moment later Jillian shouted, "Good gravy!"

"I know!" Savannah hollered back.

"What? *What?*" Lenora demanded. "And keep your voices down. Some folks in this house are trying to sleep."

"Did you click on that one link?"

Savannah nodded, reading her screen with an increasingly horrified expression. "Jillian. He's a *felon*."

Lenora put down her knitting. "What has got into you two?"

Jillian swallowed hard and passed her the phone. "Read that."

Lenora snatched it out of her hand with a glare and an unintelligible mutter. As she read her eyes grew big.

"Say what?" She read it again, then grabbed the photo and scrutinized it once more. She lifted her gaze and looked ill. "Rick Drummond is Richard Earl Drumm?"

"So it seems," Jillian said grimly.

"What in the world is he up to, sniffing around The Chocolate Shoppe like he's been doing?" Lenora scowled at the photo again as if expecting it to speak.

Jillian got up. "Savannah, we have to go after him."

"I agree."

"Whatever he has in mind can't be good." She curled and uncurled her hands.

"Mercy." Lenora took off her glasses and rubbed her eyes. "I always said a handsome man is a dangerous thing." She pointed at the phone. "And this proves it. We gotta protect your grandma. I got a feelin' Rick Drummond has something up his sleeve."

"I got a feeling you are right. Do either of you know where he lives?" Jillian asked them.

"Not a clue," Lenora said.

"I saw his car outside the Raindrop Motel once," Savannah said.

"That dump." Jillian sighed and plopped back down on the sofa. "If I'd seen it parked there, I would've thought he was helping someone who was down on their luck. He really had us all going, didn't he?"

"He's probably staying there," Lenora said. "That's the kind of place people of his ilk hole up. I wonder how long he's been out of the lockup."

Savannah looked up from her phone. "It says he has been in and out of prison his entire life. Burglary, aggravated assault, fraud, not to mention all kinds of misdemeanors."

"A career criminal," Lenora whispered.

"This piece says he pretended to be a visiting minister in Kansas, preached a sermon one Sunday, and disappeared after the potluck dinner with that day's tithes and offerings. Apparently pretending to be something he isn't to get money out of folks is how he makes his living when he's not in jail."

"And we all thought Moss Hollow had been blessed he was settling here." Jillian's head swam and she felt sick.

"Your poor grandma. Mercy, mercy." Lenora took Jillian's hand and squeezed it.

"He took us all in," Savannah said.

"Smooth-talking snake," Jillian muttered. Her thoughts circled back to her embezzling ex-fiancé, David Drake—the reason she had lost her job and her life in California and returned to Moss Hollow—but she refused to let them settle and roost there. "I've had more than enough snakes in my life."

"So what're we going to do?" Lenora asked.

"We're going to stop him before he causes us or anybody else more trouble, that's what," Jillian jumped up. "As soon as I put on my sneakers."

She bounded upstairs, slid off her comfy slippers and put on sneakers that had gel insoles and good arch support. She had a feeling she was going to need that comfort.

"Savannah?" she called as she headed back down the stairs. "How about borrowing an outfit and shoes instead of going after Rick Drummond in your dress and flats? Here. Change quick." She tossed her friend a pair of jeans, a long-sleeved T-shirt, and another pair of sneakers.

"I'm coming with you," Lenora said, packing away her knitting.

"You should stay here," Jillian said. "Keep an eye on Bertie and Aunt Cornelia. If either of them gets up for any reason, try to get them back to bed quickly. Don't tell them anything about

Rick. They don't need to know anything that will disturb their sleep tonight. And if that man comes calling, don't let him in the house. Tell him we all have chicken pox or something, then call the police and text me."

"If I'd be more help that way, I'll stay." Lenora glanced at the overnight case near her feet. "I'm all set."

Jillian remembered the pistol. *Oh dear.*

"Just be careful," she said, "and don't get hurt."

"Ain't nobody ever got me yet, and they ain't gonna do it tonight."

"Keep your phone in your pocket."

"Roger that. Ten-four." She patted the pocket of her floral lavender jacket.

"We aren't really cops or detectives," Jillian said.

"I know, but in a case like this, I can talk like we are, can't I?"

Jillian felt a rush of warmth for the woman and impulsively planted a kiss on her soft cheek. "I'm unsure how they really talk, but if they say 'roger' and 'ten-four', then go for it. See you later."

In the car a few minutes later, Savannah said, "What's your plan?"

"I don't have one."

"We can't just—"

"We have to 'just.' There's no time for plotting and planning. If he wants The Chocolate Shoppe for whatever reason, he won't waste time. So we're flying by the seat of our pants."

"I don't like the sound of that."

"Sorry, but it's all we have right now."

Savannah drove silently for a moment. "What if we call the sheriff's office?"

"And tell them what? I know we're right, but Gooder or even Laura Lee would say that we have little to go on. Just an old photograph and some Internet searches."

"Then let's brainstorm. Let's see if we can find him—"

"That sounds like a plan."

"—and when we find him, we talk to him."

"Now that does *not* sound like a plan," Jillian said. "'Say, Rick, you're a lying, deceitful snake in the grass, so why are you in Moss Hollow and what are your intentions for The Chocolate Shoppe?' Is that what you mean?"

"No, that's not what I mean. He likes you, Jillian, so you—"

"Hold it right there, buckaroo. He does not like me. He's only been flirting with me because he wants something from us."

"Nope. If all he wants is to get his hands on the bakery, he would keep working on Bertie and Cornelia. He likes you. Really likes you."

"You are turning my stomach."

"And if he thinks he is winning you over, then getting the bakery would be that much easier. You and The Chocolate Shoppe. That's what he wants."

They entered the city limits and started looking for Rick's mud-colored sedan. A drive past the Raindrop Motel showed them only an older-model pickup and a dented station wagon in the parking lot. A drive around the building turned up nothing else.

They drove up and down the streets and scoured every parking lot.

"Look at that." Savannah pointed toward Confections & Donuts as they passed. "Closed. I would have thought they would stay open twenty-four hours."

Jillian looked at the bakery, devoid of activity, security lights giving off a soft blue emanation.

"You think Rick has been in cahoots with those people?"

Savannah took her eyes off the road to give Jillian an odd look. "I never thought of that. Of course, until this evening, I never thought of Rick as being some sort of crook."

Neither spoke for a while. As they drove along the block on Main Street where The Chocolate Shoppe sat, Jillian gazed at the darkened building with a lump in her throat. The brick building, the aged glass that was a little wavy, the front door leading into the dear old bakery with its warmth and familiar scents, that beloved place where she'd spent so many hours with people who meant the most to her. No one was going to take it from her family, no matter what she had to do.

"Savannah!" She sat straight up and peered hard into the darkness. "I think someone is behind the bakery."

"What did you see?"

"I think I saw a light back there. Like a flashlight."

"Doesn't Bertie have motion-sensor lights at the back door?"

She shook her head. "There's a light above it, but the switch is inside next to the door."

Savannah turned on the next street, and as they neared the alley that ran behind The Chocolate Shoppe and other businesses, Jillian strained her eyes to see anyone or anything out of the ordinary.

"There's his car," she said. "Don't drive down the alley or he'll see us. Park somewhere else and we'll sneak up on him."

They parked a couple of blocks away, grateful that the blocks were short in Moss Hollow. They reached the back of The Chocolate Shoppe quickly.

"Let's turn off the flashlights on our phones. I want to see what he's doing before he knows we're here."

"Honestly, Jillian, don't you think we should call the cops?" Savannah turned off the light.

"We will, but not yet. We need proof. Come on."

Glad they'd worn sneakers, they crept along the side of the building toward the back.

"Look at that light moving around back there," Savannah whispered.

"I hear scraping."

"Me too. What on earth is he doing?"

"We're going to find out in a second."

They reached the corner. Careful not to make a sound, Jillian peeked around it. The alley was dimly lit by stars and a quarter moon, and they stayed hidden away from the streetlights. Rather than attempting to break into the bakery through the back door as Jillian had expected, Rick had set two small LED lanterns on the ground nearby and was gouging the dirt around the concrete stoop with a pry bar. They watched him in mystified silence for a bit.

"What is he doing?" Savannah's words were a mere breath that stirred near Jillian's ear.

"I have no idea, but we're going to find out." She stepped away from the building and turned her phone's flashlight on him. "What are you up to, Rick?"

He jumped like he'd been shot and looked toward them. He held up one hand to shield his eyes from the bright light.

"Who's that?" he said.

"It's Jillian."

"And Savannah." She stepped up beside Jillian.

"Well, hello, ladies. What're you doing here?" He displayed his familiar smile—the same warm, personal smile that seemed to disarm so many. But in the glare of both flashlights now trained on him, they could see his unease, how he darted glances all around as if looking for an escape.

"The question is, what are *you* doing here?" Jillian asked.

"I'm, uh . . . hey, I hate to admit to being so careless, but I lost my wallet earlier." He gave a forced laugh and patted his pockets. "I thought maybe it might be out here."

"You lost your wallet behind the bakery?" No one could mistake the disbelief in Savannah's voice.

"I helped Bertie take out the trash earlier, so it could have fallen out then."

The explanation seemed reasonable enough, except that the shop had been closed that day, and the method he was using for his search seemed excessive.

"So you're looking for it with a crowbar?" Jillian said. "And a sledgehammer and a shovel? That must be some wallet."

He lost his charming smile. "What are you saying, Jillian?"

"I'm saying this situation is as fishy as all get-out."

"I'm calling the cops." Savannah's screen illuminated her face.

"Why, you little—" Rick lunged, swinging the crowbar.

The phone flew from Savannah's grasp, and he grabbed her as she tried to retrieve it.

Savannah screamed and struggled as Rick growled and cursed, pinning her arms and trying to take her to the ground.

Jillian pressed 911 on her own phone and yelled into it when the operator answered. "This is Jillian Green and I'm being attacked by a man behind The Chocolate Shoppe!" She dropped the phone, leaving the line open. "Leave her alone!" she shrieked and leaped on his back.

She wrapped her legs around his torso and dug her nails into his face and scalp. He howled and let go of Savannah as he tried to fight off Jillian. Savannah tumbled to the ground, but scrambled up and hurled herself at him from behind. All three hit the ground. Breathless and obviously in pain, Rick was incapacitated long enough for Jillian to settle on his back and position herself so his arms were immobile in her rage-fueled grip. Savannah sat on his legs and ground his knees into the gravel. He soon gained his breath and tried to get up, but they were fully committed to keeping him facedown in the dirt.

They welcomed the sound of sirens and the approaching flash of lights.

20

Belle Haven's new kitchen fairly burst with admiring friends.

"And these are repurposed cabinets?" Annalise Reed ran a well-manicured hand over the smooth white paint.

"Nearly everything in here is repurposed, salvaged, and renovated." Bertie beamed in a way Jillian hadn't seen for weeks. The haunted look in her eyes was gone, along with the dark smudges beneath them.

"I love the appliances," Savannah said. "They remind me of the ones that were in my great-grandmother's kitchen."

"Grant Bower bent over backward for us," Bertie said. "Not only was he able to find rebuilt vintage appliances and cabinets, he was able to get us a great deal on these countertops. They are made from recycled glass. And these beautiful floors are salvaged walnut from an old hotel in Brunswick."

"Gordon helped too," Cornelia added. "That boy knows about conservation and recycling."

Gordon stood somewhat apart from the group, smiling, watching, and saying little. He flushed at the mention of his name. "It was my pleasure to have helped you, Miss Bertie and Miss Cornelia. And you, Jillian."

Jillian felt a pang of guilt about the way she'd suspected their reclusive friend and neighbor of suspicious behavior. She traded a glance with Savannah and wondered if she felt the same.

"I think it's disgraceful the way that Rick person tried to hoodwink everyone," Wanda Jean said.

"If you'd killed your best friend and buried him in a back parking lot twenty years ago, wouldn't you want to get rid of the evidence when it looked like someone was about to discover the remains when they expanded the building?" Cornelia asked.

"Don't tell me you're still soft about him. He's a murderer!" Bertie glowered at her. "And now that the law knows about it, he'll spend the rest of his days behind bars."

"I'm not soft about him or anyone else," Cornelia countered. "I'm just pointing out that if word hadn't gotten out that we were thinking of expanding the shop, he wouldn't have shown up and caused the mess he did."

"Breaking in and putting spoiled food in the kitchen was bad enough," Lenora said, "but turning rats loose . . ." She shuddered. "If he hadn't been so experienced at breaking and entering, I might have heard him."

"I'm glad you didn't hear him, Lenora," Bertie said. "You might have ended up like poor Chuck Stanifer. They found his bones under that concrete stoop by the back door. To think there's been a body out there since that plumbing accident all those years ago." She shuddered. "Earl and Chuck were so nice when they fixed it, and they were the best of friends. I never would have suspected that either of them had it in him to kill the other. Apparently they had been out drinking the night it happened, and Earl killed Chuck in a drunken fit of rage over something stupid. I can't believe Cornelia and I didn't recognize Earl when he came back as Rick. If Rick had succeeded in digging him up and getting rid of his remains, he would have gotten clean away."

"His experience as a crook and a thief is how he got into Belle Haven and set the kitchen on fire," Cornelia said. "I'm glad he didn't murder us."

"I believe he was trying to convince us one way or another to sell the place to him so no one would find poor Chuck Stanifer's remains out back," Jillian said. "I don't think he wanted to kill or injure us, but he seemed to think that by setting fire to our kitchen, we'd be forced to spend all our savings getting it repaired. Then we'd be so desperate that we'd be grateful for him taking The Chocolate Shoppe off our hands."

"What a dirty, sneaky trick!" Maudie said.

"He doesn't know us very well, does he, Jillian?" Bertie said.

"We are a stubborn lot in this family," she admitted. "That's not going to change."

"What did you do with that lovely new fridge he gave you?" Lucille Ryder, one of Cornelia's garden club friends, asked.

"That went back to the rental place where he'd gotten it," Bertie said. "We had to pay the rental fees, because he told Jim Wells, the manager, that I'd agreed to pay them when it was time to bring the refrigerator back. Jim knows me and trusts me, and I reckon he believed Rick. I declare that young man is a slick talker. He can make anyone believe him."

"Let's hope he gets a tough judge and jury," Annalise said.

For a while, everyone chatted with one another, then Wanda Jean spoke up.

"Have you heard the latest about Confections & Donuts?"

Jillian groaned inside. Trust Wanda Jean to bring up something that was bound to get Bertie on edge all over again. Alyce and Breanna Sherman had attended a couple of the Sweetie Pies meetings and had been quite pleasant. Much to the credit of other women, the two had been treated with courtesy, if a bit of wariness. But they hadn't been present at the most recent meeting.

"Don't start another rumor, please," Savannah said.

"This is not a rumor. If you ever listened to news radio like I do, you'd hear it there." She paused and looked around. "I take it none of you know about it, then?"

"For heaven's sake," Maudie snapped. "Don't make such a big production. We're all tired of big productions."

It was the first time Jillian had ever heard Maudie get short with her friend. Wanda Jean favored Maudie with a cool stare, then turned to the others.

"They are bankrupt."

Complete silence fell.

"Since when?" Bertie asked. "I never heard a word about it."

"I only heard this morning, but likely it'll be all over the news by now."

Jillian and Savannah got busy on ther phones.

"She's right," Savannah said. "Here is an item from a financial website that I use all the time in my business. It seems that the parent company was trying to grow too fast, opening up franchises in smaller markets all over the country. They stretched their capital and their supply chains too thin and have had to file for insolvency. The Sherman sisters were caught in the middle of it all. They've had to close the Moss Hollow bakery to concentrate on the ones in the bigger Texas market."

"Did you ever?" Cornelia said. "That just goes to show you."

Everyone looked at her.

"Goes to show you what, Aunt Cornelia?" Jillian prodded when it seemed she would say no more.

"You can't trust strangers."

"That's not completely true," Savannah said. "How would you ever make new friends if you didn't trust someone you just met?"

"Be that as it may, your home, your hometown, your friends—no stranger can take that love and trust from you."

Wanda Jean cleared her throat. Her face was flushed and she fidgeted, first fingering the top button on her blouse, then smoothing her thick knot of white hair.

"Speaking of that. There's just one more little thing that you should know." She carefully avoided all of their gazes. Jillian had never seen the woman act this way.

"Don't look at me," Maudie held up both hands as every eye turned to her. "I haven't the foggiest notion what she's talking about."

Wanda Jean shifted and cleared her throat again. She looked down at her hands and twisted a paper napkin into a hard little spear. "You don't know about it, Maudie, because I didn't tell you. I've been too ashamed."

The two women were practically joined at the hip. If Wanda Jean hadn't shared something with Maudie, the information must be uniquely remarkable. Jillian's interest sharpened. The silence was so complete in the room that it nearly hurt her eardrums.

"Here's the thing." She paused again.

"I wish you'd get to it, whatever it is," Lenora prodded.

"A while back I ran into Leslie Phipps at the library."

"Lucky you," someone muttered, drawing light laughter.

Wanda Jean kept her gaze on the twisted tissue in her hands. "You know how Leslie is. I'm not trying to pass judgment or anything, but it's hard to get away from her."

"She will talk your arm off, if you let her," Cornelia said, nodding.

"Go on, Wanda Jean," Jillian said.

"Anyway, she was going on and on about Confections & Donuts and how much the town needed big business, even if it was a bakery. And I don't know why, but Bertie, before I could stop myself, I was telling her how upset you'd been and how unlike yourself, and about you talking with Grant, and how you might sell the place or close it down, well—"

"Wanda Jean Maplewood, are you saying Leslie Phipps wrote that article in the newspaper?" Bertie demanded.

"If she didn't, she knows who did, because she's the only one I told."

The silence turned uncomfortable and Wanda Jean stopped fidgeting. She clenched the napkin tightly in one hand and didn't look up.

"I'm sorry, Bertie. I should've come clean with you before now, but I was just so ashamed and embarrassed. Then Jillian got kinda high and mighty with us, and I felt even worse." She cut a quick glance at Jillian.

"Excuse me." Savannah left the room.

Bertie drew in a deep breath and blew it out as noisily as a pressure tank. "You know what?" she said. "I'm plumb worn out. In fact, I'm beyond worn out. I'm down to a nub. And I'm ready, willing, and able to put this whole mess behind me if we can all just get back to our lives."

"I think that's the best idea I've heard in a good long time," Jillian said.

"Amen, honey." Lenora beamed at her. "It's time to be our normal selves living our normal lives."

"I'm willing if y'all are," Cornelia said. Everyone agreed with enthusiasm.

Jillian stood. "How about some refills of sweet tea?"

"And we've still got doughnuts." Lenora fetched the box and passed them around while Jillian topped off everyone's drinks.

Savannah came back after several minutes. "I just had an enlightening chat on the phone with Leslie." All talking stopped and every eye turned to her. "I called and flat-out asked her if she wrote that article. She admitted she did and kept trying to change the subject, but I held a tight rein on the conversation. The upshot of it is Leslie not only wrote that article, but she was the author of that letter to the editor from Jimmie-June Jessup."

"Why on earth?" Cornelia screeched. "Is she out of her mind?"

"I think we can safely assume Leslie Phipps is rarely in full control of herself," Savannah said.

"But what about the vandalism and threats Alyce and Breanna received?" Jillian said. "Surely Leslie had no hand in that."

"She says not. That wouldn't make a lick of sense."

"Nobody ever said that girl had a lick of sense."

"Let's not get nasty," Bertie chided. "She was just doing what she thought she needed to do to have friends. That's always been her trouble anyway—her desperation to be liked."

"Apparently she was so eager to please Megan, who has been such a proponent of Confections & Donuts, that Leslie thought she was being an invaluable help to her and to Moss Hollow."

"With help like that, who needs plagues of locusts, droughts, and famine?" Lenora asked.

"Bless her heart," Bertie said softly, shaking her head. "Makes you wonder if she will ever have a close friend, someone she can trust and who can trust her."

Everyone was silent for a bit. Jillian thought of Leslie, so overeager in school, trying out for cheerleader, running for class officer, joining every club she could, and yet never fitting in. The lack of acceptance made her try that much harder and, as a result, alienated her even more.

"I'm glad they found those two young hooligans who started the fire on Guy & Ginger's," Cornelia said. "Only twelve years old and up to those kinds of shenanigans. Can you imagine?"

"It wasn't so much a case of finding them as their conscience bothering both of them so much that they told their parents," Savannah said. "They didn't do it on purpose. They were just irresponsible with the wrong tools."

"I hope they learned their lesson."

"I heard rumors that some folks thought I set the fire and vandalized that property, but I hope you know me well enough to know I'm all about peace and preservation, not wanton destruction." Gordon had been so quiet Jillian had nearly forgotten his presence.

"We know that." She smiled at him.

"We still don't know who wrote the notes to those Sherman women."

"I doubt anyone is going to own up to it," Cornelia said.

"I heard that they did it themselves just to stir up sympathy," Wanda Jean, ever the gossip, inserted.

"Now don't you start," Maudie said. "Let's give bad feelings a break, can't we?"

"I don't think Alyce and Breanna are as bad as everyone thought they were. And remember, they've lost their livelihood now, or at least part of it." Jillian passed a look around. "Like we almost did. So let's keep them in our prayers. They need friends too."

The phone rang, interrupting the conversation.

Cornelia looked at her watch. "Just as I expected. I'll get it. Listen to this, y'all."

Everyone looked at one another, mystified. She picked up the receiver of the phone on the counter.

"Hello?" A pause that lasted a few seconds. "No, Teresa is not here, and I'm not giving you any money, but honey, let me tell you something. I have been having the worst ache in my toes. I have corns. Do you have corns? Well, corns and bunions are the bane of old feet, and when you get to be my age—no, no, I'm talking, so you listen to me. I had gallbladder surgery once, and you should have seen the gallstones they removed. Why, I bet—wait, wait. You don't have to hang up yet, because I'm not finished, and I haven't had anyone to talk to today. Let me tell you what my doctor said about this rash under my arm once it started oozing—" She held the phone to her ear a moment longer, her mischievous grin spreading wider and wider across her face. She hung up the phone and turned to the others.

"Aunt Cornelia, was that the guy you mentioned before, the one who calls all the time?"

"The scammer who asks for Teresa? Sure was. He calls three or four times a week at this time of day, and I can't just let a phone ring like Jillian wants me to do. It makes me twitch. I put Belle

Haven's number on the no-call list, but that didn't help. So I told him every time to stop calling. I have tried to reason with him, but he won't listen. Sometimes I pick up the receiver and hang it right back up. But it occurred to me a minute ago that if I were to rattle on like Leslie does, I might wear him out and he'll quit calling. So let's see if he calls again in a day or two."

"Maybe he needs a friend too." Annalise said with a twinkle in her eye, but such a serious expression on her face that Cornelia blinked at her.

"You think that's why he calls people all day long and tries to scam them out of their money? You think he's looking for a friend that way?"

Annalise's somber expression faded and the smile in her eyes filled her face. "Maybe. More than likely, though, he's just trying to make money any way he can."

Possum strolled into the kitchen, tail high, ignoring everyone as he headed toward his food bowl. Cornelia watched him.

"I'm sorry, but I need to go. It's time for Raymond's supper." She paused, head slightly tilted, thinking. "When you get right down to it, what we all need and want is to have friends and be a friend, isn't it?"

"It sure is," Maudie said. "Why, Wanda Jean and I have been pals since we were knee-high to a grasshopper."

"All I can say is I'm glad I have all y'all in my life," Bertie said, "and I know my sister feels the same way."

"Yes, I do." The twins gave each other identical smiles.

"We all do," Jillian added.

Sweet Sabotage
Book Nine Recipe

Bertie's Pecan Sticky Buns

Dough

1 package active dry yeast
¼ cup warm water (105 to 115 degrees F)
¼ cup milk, scalded then cooled to lukewarm

¼ cup sugar
1 egg, beaten
¼ cup vegetable shortening
2¼ to 2½ cups self-rising flour

Filling

2 tablepoons butter, softened
¼ cup sugar

2 teaspoons cinnamon

Topping

½ cup butter, melted
½ cup light-brown sugar

½ cup pecan halves

Instructions

1. For dough, in a large mixing bowl, dissolve yeast in warm water.

2. Add milk, sugar, egg, and shortening, stirring until shortening is melted and ingredients are incorporated.

3. Add half the flour; stir with spoon until well blended. Add remaining flour gradually and stop when dough is easy to handle.

4. Turn mixture onto floured board and knead for five minutes, or until smooth and elastic. Place in greased bowl, turning so greased dough surface is at the top.

5. Cover bowl and let dough rise in a warm place until doubled, about 1½ hours. Punch down dough and let rest 10 minutes.

6. Roll dough on a lightly floured board into a 15 x 9-inch rectangle.

1. For filling, spread softened butter over surface of dough rectangle.

2. Mix sugar and cinnamon, and sprinkle evenly over buttered dough.

3. Starting at one long side, roll up the dough rectangle tightly, jelly roll–style. Press outer edge against roll to seal well. Cut roll into 15 even slices; set aside.

1. For topping, mix melted butter, brown sugar, and pecan halves. Spread evenly over bottom of a 9 x 13 x 2-inch baking pan.

2. Place roll slices in pan. Cover and let rise until double in size, about 40 minutes.

3. Preheat oven to 375 degrees. Bake 25 to 30 minutes, or until lightly golden on top.

Up to this point, we've been doing all the writing. Now it's *your* turn!

Tell us what you think about this book, the characters, the bad guy, or anything else you'd like to share with us about this series. We can't wait to hear from *you*!

Log on to give us your feedback at:
https://www.surveymonkey.com/r/ChocolateShoppe